WORDS

TO

READ

Charles Schwend

Quill To Book Publishing

Words To Read

Copyright 2019 by Charles Schwend

Covers

Copyright 2019 by Charles Schwend

ISBN: 978-0-9966512-7-1

Other Books Written by Charles Schwend

<u>Dragon Dreams</u> – A beautiful young woman; An intimidating old man; An ugly dragon; A mysterious sword; A mythology from the dawn of time. All challenge the sanity of an unwilling young sailor selected to become the leader of a secret organization that is over two thousand years old. While stationed at an old Kamikaze base, he saves an old man, with a secret life, from a frozen river. His valiant rescue empowers him by ancient mandate, to become the Master of the White Ninja, a position he does not understand, nor want. The story is a tapestry of myth, love, danger and death. Dragon Dreams will capture an open mind in a novel of historical fact and mythological accuracy. This is not a book of martial arts.

<u>Words To Read, A Collection of Short Stories</u> – A colorful, insightful, collection of 23 memoirs, stories and one poem, based on recollection, legend and fantasy. The writings stem from Schwend's experience in the U.S. Navy, hobbies, family, and observing the world around him. Fantasy and a vivid imagination provide the mental stimulation for the remaining words to entertain an inquisitive mind. The short stories are from true memoirs, observation, whimsical half truths to full out fictional whim.

<u>Gulag #7, The Authorized Biography of Karl Lawrenz</u> - A gritty account of Karl Lawrenz from birth in Pomerania, Germany to his current retirement as a U.S. Citizen, living in Highland, IL. This book is about his life and internment in a Siberian Gulag (POW camp) during WWII when he was 15 years old. He nearly died many times from starvation and illness. After WWII he continued to suffer under the harsh Russian rule of slave labor. He credits God for his life; his wife Inge, for the happiness found in his life; and the U.S. for the quality of his subsequent life. Some memories are a little grey. Karl cannot be one hundred

percent sure that all his recall is without error. Some may not be remembered for a reason, or a purpose.

<u>The Magical Switch</u> – Originally written for a poetry contest sponsored by Famous Poets Institute and won an Honorable Mention from over seven thousand entries. The poem was written for a bedtime reading to assist young children to overcome their fear of sleeping in the dark. The book illustrations were made by Nicole Dormeier.

<u>The Palace of Virtual Reality</u> – A Professor Hamlock, head of a university science department, discovers how to bring holograms to life. Merlin the magician is the first to be re-created, followed by Aphrodite and other Greek Gods. Murder, lust, adventure and mystery soon follows.

<u>Words, An Anthology of Short Writings</u> - Editor of and Contributing Author.

<u>Homemade Cordials, Better Than Bought</u> – This book will enable the reader to successfully make a good quality cordial to their liking, with basic equipment. To improve their cordial making skills and blend, bottle, age, share and enjoy the fruits of their creativity. Anyone can make his or her own cordials that will rival anything that can be bought.

<u>The Keys, And Other Short Stories</u> is a collection of short stories that will entertain readers of every genre. Readers have acclaimed the individual stories as excellent reading. The Keys will be especially appreciated by readers that want to enjoy a short story, put the book down, and return at a later time to start a new story.

<u>A Dark and Stormy Night</u> – Contributing Author

Dedication

To my wife Dolores, who suffered through the many tales told from my memories and dark recesses of my mind. Some consistent and some embellished with deeds of adventure. Some inconsistent and laced with whimsy. All written to entertain.

WORDS

TO

READ

Charles Schwend

Quill To Book Publishing

Table of Content

A Traveler's Tale

Eating a late breakfast at the Parkview Café, Marine, IL, I was talking with the owner, Kathy, when a couple of travelers entered. We were the only customers. That fact alone made it unusual since the Parkview is always busy. It must have something to do with the weather. They look a little weather beaten; nervous like a spooked horse in an unfamiliar setting.

The temperature is hitting 80 degrees, the sun is shining, and a gentle breeze massages the tree leaves, but the couple sitting at the next table look like they had just finished a stroll through a cold reefer. They are a younger couple, maybe in their late twenties. He was dressed in comfortable tan pants and a button down short sleeve shirt. Dark brown eyes matched his burr cut hair.

Her blue eyes complimented the short summer cut blonde hair. She wore white shorts and a light pink halter. Pink toes peek out of white sandals at the bottom of dropdead legs.

The waitress, Lois, walked up to their table and asked, "What would you like to drink?"

They both answered, "Iced tea."

"I'll be back to take your order," the waitress said.

The young lady stares at her partner sitting across the table. A tear trickles down her cheek. "John," she said, "we have to tell someone. We have to find someone who will believe us."

The waitress returned with their tea. "Are you ready to order?"

"No," they replied, "we will just have tea for now."

Clearing my throat to get their attention, I said, "I'm sorry, but I could not help but overhear you. I hope I am not intruding, but is there something I could help you with?"

They exchanged nervous glances. "Yes," she said, "maybe you can. This is my fiancé John Cablis, and I am Trudy White. We have a frightening story that we cannot keep to ourselves anymore."

"My grandparents, George and Sally White lived near Highland, on Silver Creek. The land had been in our family since before the area was settled. George had always told me, when I was a visiting, that he had a map to a hoard of silver passed down to him from his great-grandfather. The treasure came from an old silver mine. The silver was buried during an Indian uprising. The wounded mule skinners who buried the silver made their way to George's ancestor's cabin. Before they died, they drew the map for him, explaining the landmarks on the map, and the dangers that would be encountered retrieving the silver. He also told of a young Indian maiden that was buried with the silver, following old superstition, for her spirit to protect the treasure. He had told many people of his map, but they all thought he was just story telling. He never came across as being very credible.

"My grandmother Sally died 10 years ago. Grandfather George spent the last 3 years of his life in a nursing home, telling the story to all that would listen. I guess he needed attention, and the story made him feel important. Two weeks ago, his doctor told him he was dying, he sent for me. He told me where he hid the old map. When he had to move to a new cabin when Silver Lake was built, a water tight safe room was built under the smokehouse with access through a concrete slab in the floor.

`"For the past week John and I have been out at Silver Lake looking for the site of Grandfather George's cabin. We were informed it was demolished when the new property owners started to build their home. We finally discovered the location through the plats and deeds office, at the courthouse in Edwardsville. But we do not know where the smokehouse was standing. While talking to the current owner, we found out the smokehouse was burned down, the area leveled and landscaped. We don't think it would be smart to inform the current land owner of the treasure; we would lose any claim to it.

"Then last night, my grandfather came to me in a dream. He told me the treasure is cursed, and that I should abandon the search for it. Why would he now tell me of the curse after all this time? I feel that there is another reason for his warning, maybe for our safety, or maybe because there is no treasure.

"We should not be dragging you into this problem. SShh, here comes the waitress," said Trudy.

"Chuck refill?" "Are you people ready to order yet?"

"Yes," I said.

The couple at the next table said "No, just a refill."

"I remember the lay of that ground. A friend of mine farmed that area until they parceled it out in five acre building lots. I'll give him a call. It will just take a minute." Pulling a cell phone from my jacket, I punch in Bill's number. He answered and I told him the information we were looking for.

He told me exactly where the old smoke house use to stand. "I was just out there last week. Why do you want to know?"

"Some relatives of old man White are in the restaurant and wants to know the whereabouts of that old building. Apparently the building is prominent in their old memories. Thanks for the info Bill," I replied.

I repeated what Bill told me, but they could not place the location in their minds. "Tell you what;

I'll take you out there early tomorrow morning," I said.

They look at each other, their eyes questioning each other. Looking back at me Trudy said, "We don't want to get you, or us, in any kind of trouble. We don't even know if this worth any risk."

"Naw, I know those people. They party late into the night, and don't rise till noon. I think we'll be safe." I told them where to meet me the next morning at 5 a.m., what to wear, and what to bring.

The next morning was dark and foggy when I saw them waiting for me at the park. Their clothes were appropriate for tramping through the woods. We packed into my trusty 4-wheel drive truck, John in the passenger seat and Trudy in the jump seat with the extra equipment, food and coffee. They both had a grim look and did not speak, not even light talk. Approaching a field road, I said, "Here's where we cut back into the woods. We'll come into the property the back way. No one will see or hear us. Remember, sounds carry a long way in this

8

heavy air. The fog should be thicker where we're going. Trudy, you carry the mantle lantern. John and I will each carry a spade and I'll also take a probe."

John grunts, and Trudy nods. We pick up our equipment from the truck bed and start walking through the tall grass soaked from the fog. We follow the field road for about fifteen minutes until we reach the rise. "Bill said the smokehouse was about twenty five feet east of this big white oak." Pushing the spade blade into the ground so I would not trip over it in the grass, I eased the 6 foot probe down, searching for concrete. I probed in a grid, every six foot in each direction. After thirty minute I found myself tiring and John took over when he saw me slowing down. Another twenty minutes passed until I heard the probe thunk on something hard. John gave me a surprised look. "Probe all around it, and go out a foot in all directions to make sure it's not just a rock." Each new probe produced the welcomed thunk.

Trudy giggled. John suppressed an excited laugh. Without speaking, John and I pick up our spades and start to dig. The soil was loose and easily worked after we passed through the sod. It was another thirty five minutes before we scraped the dirt off the concrete slab. The fog was starting to lift but it was not light enough to put out the lamp. We still could not see the new house on the property, or hear anyone stirring. There are no traffic noises, no dogs barking.

John stubbed his shoe on a large iron ring imbedded in a three foot square block. I thought we would break the spade handle that we put through the ring, to lift the block of concrete. We both groan in our efforts. Finally, with an ominous scraping, the block rose from the slab. I could almost hear the fresh cool air pour into the dark hole. I pulled a flashlight from it's holder on my belt, shined it down into the dark void at our feet. The floor was wet; looked slippery with a coating of mud. Kneeling, I sweep the beam around the walls.

Wooden shelves rested on cinder blocks holding gallon canning jars that contained rolled up yellowed papers sealed inside. John sat on the edge of the opening and slid down to the floor. Trudy followed with John holding her legs, letting her slide down into his arms until they encircle her waist. Positioning myself to follow Trudy, I heard someone speak.

"That won't be necessary Chuck. Just stay where you are." Bill walked out of the undergrowth. He was holding a pistol with a silencer, motioning me back away from the opening with a flashlight in his other hand. He walked up to the opening, shined the light beam down into the black void. He introduced himself, and then ordered Trudy to find the map.

"What are you doing?" asked John.

"Just lining my retirement basket. Get busy, do what I want and no one will get hurt. All I want is the silver. Old man White told me that treasure story a hundred times," said Bill. "If anyone is entitled to it, it's me. Get busy, get me that map. Hurry up, the fog is breaking up. If I don't get the map, I'll leave but you won't."

"We're hurrying. Most of the jar screw caps are rusty and won't budge," said Trudy.

"Break the damn jars. Do what ever you have to do, just find that damn map," Bill ordered, and then looked at me. "I don't believe you will leave this place Chuck, you know too much. You're too much of a liability."

John cried out. "We found it, we found it here."

"Pass it up idiot," said Bill

I started to bend down to help John and Trudy up when a blow to the back of my head caused me to fall into the hole. I felt John and Trudy try to catch me, to break my fall. Half conscious I heard the block scrape shut above me. Water poured over my face and into my mouth. Coughing, I struggled to my feet. Pulling out my flashlight, I told Trudy to turn off the lantern, to conserve our oxygen.

Panning the walls with the light beam revealed a small square wooden door, half way up the concrete wall, and behind a section of shelving. "This may be our way out, help me move this stuff...," I said. In fifteen minutes, the boards and cinder blocks are moved out of the way. The stuck door was pried open with the help of a shelf board. The tunnel was bricked out but almost choked shut with roots and spider webs. Moving through the tunnel, we dead end at another wooden panel. I kicked the panel out to find fresh air. The fog had lifted and a bright moon illuminated a deep ditch running past a large root ball, just above my head. Pushing out, I rolled to the bottom of the ditch. John and Trudy followed.

Bill must have taken time to study the map. He was crashing through the underbrush. Putting a finger to my lips, I motion upward with my other hand. They nod with acknowledgement; they too heard Bill thrashing through the brush. A loud scream echoed through the woods. Scrambling up the side of the ditch, we spread out and head toward the source of the scream.

We find Bill dead, lying in the entrance of an old cave that was overgrown with brush. There was a splintered arrow with ratty fletching sticking out of his chest. Pulling Bill out of the entrance, we shined our flashlights into the dark hole. There was a skeleton covered with a decayed deerskin dress, holding a shattered bow, resting on a pile of silver ingots.

Knoll Mansion

The old Mansion sat on a lonely knoll, not quite tall enough to be called a hill, but high enough to enable a view of the surrounding land. Not a living thing grew for one mile distance in any direction. Hardpan clay and gravel made the ground hard and weatherproof. The winter freeze could not heave or soften the surface with thaw.

Family legend says that the old building stands four stories high, with a ten foot attic space, and no one knows how many levels lie beneath the basement. It seems the house howls and moans with the slightest breeze. It was made from boulders and stone that came from an unreasonable distance. The walls were mortared with a type of crushed lime that makes the surface appear to be solid rock.

Only after viewing the basement interior, does one realize that the building was built on a pre-existing foundation. The twelve foot basement walls have many sealed portals. Only the stone frames indicate where the doors were. There is only one door opening on each level leading to stone steps going down to the next sub-level. The lightest step, with the softest of footwear, produces scratchy echoes that forewarn all that lie below. No one has reported to have ever reached the bottom level, or should I say no living person.

Family legends of an unknown beautiful woman who haunts the house came to mind. Her ghost has kept vandals and curious treasure seekers from entering and corrupting the presence of the home since its construction. An ill feeling invades all unwelcome guests. An invitation to leave is sensed spiritually as an aggressive thought.

When entering the house through the front entrance, one views a grand staircase growing from the main floor, rising up through the second and third, ending at an equally grand landing on the fourth. Each floor has a different flourish of décor from different periods of history.

There is a heavy chill through out, even in the warmest season, as though the house controls the temperature and humidity, without mechanical means. One can almost understand what the house was trying to say, if only they would still themselves and listen intently.

As the last of my family, I have been charged with describing the property and contents for auction. Having never being inside, but just hearing descriptions of the interior from prior visitors, I was reluctantly forced to enter and record inventory and my viewings.

The probate attorney had been eager to put the massive brass key to the main door in my hand. All other exterior doors had bolts, or massive sliding beams, to prevent unwanted entry.

The key, almost twelve inches long, slid into the lock easily, as if the device were permanently lubricated. The five by nine foot wooden plank door swung open smoothly, on five wrought iron hinges, each as large as my arm. Stepping inside, the heavy pungent air took my breath away, a warning against entering. I stood gasping, trying to acclimate my lungs to their new hostile environment. After a short period of recovery, a welcomed light and citrus sweetness clung to me.

Viewing the panorama that revealed itself, as my vision cleared in the dim light, my eyes locked onto the large portrait hanging above the walk-in fireplace. The larger than life woman portrayed is lifelike, more like a photograph than an exaggerated oil rendition. She is wearing a red, off the shoulder gown. Her eyes seem to follow my every movement, and her smile pulls me closer. Her image is familiar, but I can not place from where.

Stepping on a paving stone that depressed, a fire bellows up in the cavity of the fireplace. Startled, I jumped back, tripping over a table and fell to the hard floor. A crystal decanter rocked, dropped to the floor and shattered. The splintery shards cut my arm and hand. Looking up to the portrait, I saw a smile change from a sensuous to a more humorous look.

Pulling out my handkerchief, I wipe away the trickles of blood to discover the cuts have disappeared. The red blood smears on the handkerchief belie the wounds just seen. I hear a woman's soft laughter echoed down the staircase. Coldness courses through me. Looking at the portrait, I said, "Laugh all you want, I'll not be scared away from what I must do. Laugh all you want lady, whoever you are."

The smile in the portrait hardened ever so slightly, and then I hear delicate, but distinct, footsteps coming down the staircase in a slow paced rhythm. Spinning around I see an aura of descending light stop on the stair landing. Looking over my shoulder I could no longer see the woman in the portrait. A chill descends my spine, or whatever is left of my spine. The painting is complete, but without the woman.

Looking back at the foot of the staircase, I see the woman from the portrait standing there in that revealing red attire. Her hand covers her mouth as she contained a quiet laugh. Her jade green eyes sparkle in the dim light. Her youthful face shows no lines from age or hardship. Wavy auburn hair cascades down, caressing her bare shoulders. Cocking her head slightly, she said, "I have been waiting for you for a long time, more than I can remember."

"Who are you?" I asked.

"Amara, my name is Amara. Amara means eternal. Did you know that?" She said.

"No. Why have you been waiting for me?" I reply.

"We were betrothed two hundred years ago. You were murdered by an older rival suitor that my father preferred because of his wealth. I committed suicide rather than marry him. I have been waiting for you ever since," She said in soft whispering voice hinging on tears. "My prayers have been answered, my love."

She floated toward me, arms outstretched for an embrace. I stood frozen as she passed through me, then passed through me again as she backed up to face me, her mouth inches from mine. "You must embrace me, if we are to be joined together. Come put your arms around me. Show me your love," she whispered. Embracing the beautiful spirit dissolved any fear or doubt I may have harbored.

I was mesmerized. I became become a slave to her wishes. It felt as though I floated as we ascend the stairs to a bedroom on the fourth floor. The room is prepared for the threshold of marriage, a honeymoon room with plush bed, Champaign on ice, two chilled flutes, and trays of food to supplement mind, body, and soul.

Morning brings an exhaustion that I had never before known. Falling into a deep sleep, I had pleasurable dreams, reliving the forenight. In my slumber I hear a melodic voice singing in the air. No, it sounds more like an auctioneer's song, soliciting higher bids. Waking up, but my eyes still shuttered from sleep, I feel refreshed but strangely, somewhat restrained. Slowly opening my eyes, I look over the great room from above the massive fireplace to see swarms of people, milling about with numbered card in hand. Amara was standing by my side smiling. Turning my head a little more, I see we fill the portrait.

The Winner Lives

My great grandfather Charlie O'Schwend started making wine in his youth, around 1905. Raised on the family farm, he was in tune with nature, wanting to experience all that the world offered. Charlie had a leaning toward the exotic, something that no other family member had, something that made him stand out in a crowd.

Becoming a bee keeper was one hobby that he was keen on. Soon Charlie was making mead, winning top awards at the local and surrounding county fairs. His wine making reputation spread and he was invited to join the International Society of Mead Makers. Constant experimentation on the wine making process produced a vintage declared The Best in the World, true Nectar of the Gods

'The honey came from a swarm of bees that seemed to have the propensity of caring, which he returned, treating each bee as a loving friend. The main herb used was a strain of mint, only growing on the land straddling the border between his and the neighbors land. There were other secret ingredients used that he told no one, not even his family. Each year produced mead better than the year before.

The attention paid to his mead making intensified as he approached retirement years. The physical effort required, harvesting the honey, lifting the heavy barrels, and tending to the daily regimen, took its toll on his health. The last batch of mead made was only 100 gallons. Just two barrels of the exquisite amber liquid, but it had all the attributes of the finest ever made. After the last wine racking and the corks sealed with wax to prevent fluctuation pressure killing the living elixir, Charlie died. Since that time, the wine rested, aging and improving with time, in a concealed room under his home.

My father, in his youth, found and tasted the wine stored in the old sealed cellar room, and decided it should be given the respect that was its due. He found old labels his grandfather made before his death and applied them to the 500 bottles that were lovingly cared for. The bottled mead was used at all the family celebrations and gatherings. Soon word spread again of this magic drink and its effect on the mind, soul, and body. Offers to purchase came from far and wide, but the mead was not for sale. Occasionally a special person would be gifted with a bottle, carefully wrapped and packaged.

In time, I inherited the old farm, married and started a family. I do not know how, or why, my beautiful wife, Venus, decided to grace me with her loving presence. I did notice she always received double or triple appreciative glances from passing men of all ages.

Our neighbor's son, Garrett, inherited the adjoining ground and set about modernizing the tilling of the soil. During one of his rare visits I was informed of his plans to spray the borders of his property with pesticides and herbicides to eliminate the ravenous bugs and invasive weeds. When I questioned him about the bees and mint I was informed that I would have to do without them, that his rights and wants superseded mine. My loss was considered collateral damage to his needs. He further informed me that I too would have to start using modern techniques on my land or I would loose it, that he would not tolerate my weeds and pests presence to invade his ground. I replied that I would not allow him violating my legal rights.

"Well, just sit on your laurels and see what happens," he said.

Soon my dog disappeared. My mint and other ground covers withered, and my bees died. Shortly

26

after, I received a registered letter from the leading legal firm in the region, stating my neighbor was taking legal action to assume ownership of my property because of his past maintenance of the disputed land. Three days after signing for the registered letter, Garrett again visited me. Naturally I was upset with him, and his drooling stares at my wife further agitated me.

Garrett told me of his bad heart and how he must take great pains not to get excited to prevent bringing on a heart attack. I thought that if he was on the brink of death, he should not be endangering himself with his mental lusting for Venus.

Garret locked his eyes on my face, his expression was in deep thought, and he offered me a proposition. "I understand that you possess the last bottle of your father's mead, the wine that is reported to have restorative powers to one's health. If you will give me that last bottle, I will not pursue my claim on your land."

"I can not give the bottle to you," I said. "My family would not forgive me. But I could share it with you, if you would write a statement vowing never to lay claim to my land. And yes, it must be notarized, and sent to me by way of your lawyers."

We stood, and while I thought he would refuse, he stepped closer to me, shook my hand, and said, "It's a deal. I'll have the paper drawn up this day."

Four days later, his lawyer came to my door, with the document in hand. "This paper will remain in my possession until the verbal contract is consummated. Will this evening be convenient for you?"

"Yes," I replied.

"Good, Garrett and I will be here around 8:00 pm."

"The porch light will be on," I replied.

As my clock chimed 8:00 pm, there was a knock at my door. Opening the door revealed the shamus lawyer and Garrett with a triumphant look on his face.

"Inside, or shall we enjoy this lovely evening on the porch?"

"On the porch," exclaimed Garrett excitedly.

Have a seat at the table, and I will return shortly." I went to retrieve the carefully washed bottle of mead from the wine cooler, and three crystal wine goblets. Returning to the porch, I set the bottle and three glasses on the table. "Allow me," I said, picking up a cork screw. "Since I believe I still legally own this."

Carefully, and with great effort, I slowly extract the ancient cork from the bottle until a loud pop was heard. "Shall I let it breath?" I ask.

"No," said Garrett.

I carefully pour, and look into the goblet. Extending my arm over the porch railing, I tilted the goblet letting the mead cascade down, perfuming the air and the ground with its fragrance. "There were bits of cork floating," I said.

Garrett's face turned red and heavy sweat beads appear on his forehead. "What the hell do you think your doing? Give me a glass of that wine. I'll not be messing around with you. My lawyer is watching everything you do."

"Yes, I'm sure he is," I said looking into his sick eyes. I again extend my arm over the porch railing, and slowly empty the bottle. Garrett struggled to get up.

"Mr. O'Schwend, do you know what your doing?" shouted the lawyer.

The lawyer and I both turn toward the sound of a loud crash. Garrett fell across the table, slides to the floor crying out with pain, clutching his chest. The lawyer rushes to his side and checks his pulse. "You've killed him," he shouted.

"No," I said. "I just backed out of the deal."

The next day I move a hive from behind the house to the edge of my property, replanted mint from a secondary site, and went to the basement where I sat to relish the view of the wine rack filled with fifty plus bottles of the golden mead that are still left. I pick up the string bound, age yellowed, papers that I found in a hidden brick niche in a wall of the basement, my Great Grandfathers old wine log, with recipes, and started reading.

Calling for Venus to join me, I pour two glasses of wine.

Gunfight At Breakfast

Jake's gun hand trembled... He stood facing the terrible widow maker, Red. The sweat trickled down his brow, stinging his eyes. Red stared into my eyes with nary a blink, as if looking into my soul. Why, oh why, did I have to do a dang blasted dumb thing and challenge that bad ornery Red? Jake's colt 45 sat heavy in the holster. At sunrise every morning, just as regular as checking the livestock, I would free my iron from the sticky oil soaked holster. Yah, every morning; every morning but this morning. This morning was the beginning of my last day on this God's earth.

I was in my dirty cow punching clothes. I don't want to be buried in these old rags. If'n I knew what

32

stupid things I was going to do, I would have worn my Sunday clothes. Well, maybe not. If'n I knew what I might have did, I wouldn't have gone and done it. Now Red wasn't wearing old working clothes. He always sparkled in his new duds, bright bandana, and a crisp creased hat. That's what all the ladies liked about him. That and all that fancy talk he has. He doesn't have to worry about being buried in things that smell of horse and steer. That hot sun was really bringing up my week old stink. If the sun got any hotter, my eyes will water up, and I won't be able to see to shoot straight.

The morning sun was low and shining hot from over my back. Why wasn't Red squinting? His hat brim was not even shading his eyes. Was that man not human? Standing there like a scarecrow hanging on a fence post, with his arm out away from his side, relaxed, waiting for something. What dang it? What was he waiting for?

Jake's skin felt like it was crawling with biting fleas. He hates fleas, and his horse hates fleas. He knew that if he made a motion to wipe away the insects, he would be dead in less than a second. Should I make my move? Do I wait a little longer for Red to make his move? Why did I challenge him? For God's sake, it was only breakfast. I guess Red was dead serious about his breakfast.

Wait, did I see his hand twitch? What was that movement I saw? Damn, why doesn't he draw? I'm scared my eyes will never see the next sunrise. What would my sweet cake Minnie Lou think of me if I turned and ran? No, I'd never make a full step back. Red the gunslinger would have his finger on the trigger, a bullet in my heart, and my face in the dust.

Oh Lord, why did I ever put myself into this terrible pickle barrel? Red was sneering at me. No it's a smile, but I don't think it's a good smile, I can't see his teeth. Does he have teeth? He has to have something in that mouth of his in order to eat. What does he have? Why do I think of all this nonsense when I know I am going to meet my maker soon? I should be thinking of a way to get out of this mess. I should be thinking of happy times, of blue skies, beautiful mountains, a clear running river, my father, my mother, YES, my mother, my nurturing mother. What would her advice be?

Yes, I can hear her now, "Jake, you dumb pile of dung. Now look at what you have gone and done! Don't you ever do anything right? Why not just shoot Red in the back? Nobody challenges anyone anymore. You're worse than your father, that loser."

No, don't think of Mom. She would not be help. She would just tell Red to shoot me, or make him mad until he shot her, or shoot himself so he wouldn't have to hear her jawing in that scratchy voice.

I know what I'll do. I'll appeal to Red's sense of cowboy fair play. What would be fair? "Red, Red, why don't we just split it up. You take that last egg for breakfast and I'll take the bacon. We can share the toast. You can have the cup of Joe and I'll drink the sarsaparilla. How's about it Red? Do you think we can do that?"

Red wiped his chin with his dusty gloved left hand. His right hand steady just above his shooting iron. "Well, I am pretty darn hungry. I don't think I could keep an appetite after seeing a lot of blood in the street. I'll share that breakfast at the Parkview Cafe with you, since you already paid the ugly waitress."

"Ugly waitress! Ugly waitress! That's my Minnie Lou you're talking about!" Fear left my mind; my hand moves in a blur, my colt 45 aimed at Red's heart in one fast smooth motion. The crack of gunfire echoed. My vision cleared as Red hurtles backwards into the dirt, his piece still in his hand. He hit with a loud thud.

Cautiously I approached this outlaw of death. My colt was at ready to handle any dastardly action from a black heart like Red. Looking down over his stretched out body, with boot toes pointing to the sky, I saw his eyelids move. His lips parted and I heard Red say in a weakened voice.

"I think I would have rather had the bacon, and maybe some pancakes." With a slight groan, Red closed his eyes; his legs twitched a little, heels dug in the dust then he was still.

God, I hate this. Minnie Lou will have to get a different job if we are to be married. I haven't had a decent breakfast in a long time, and all this killin goes agin me.

Duke

Dolores and I were looking for a new dog to replace Blackie, who was hit and killed on the road. We wanted a dog that would take to us immediately, was energetic, and had a good bloodline and track record. We heard of a farmer with a pair of pups, who wanted to find a good home for the male. We called and made an appointment to view the little critter, and let him get acquainted with us.

We arrived at the farm to find a large, one hundred pound, leggy, black, nine month old male puppy. We could tell he liked us from the slobbers and drool he deposited on us, while trying to climb onto our laps while we were still standing. He offered us his toys; logs that were strewn around his pen. When we did not quickly respond to his offers, he laid down at our feet, rolled onto his back and looked up at us.

We were told that Duke was out of registered stock, Black Labrador and Weimaraner, with gold eyes that unlike other dogs, stared into ours. We inquired why the male was up for adoption and not the female.

"Twice," the farmer said, "He killed my chickens and placed them in a row on the lawn, and he got buckshot both times. He's a little gun shy now." The dog acted as though he knew what was being said and had the appropriate guilty look on his face. Ears drooped, head down, and looked up at us from the top of his eye sockets. His tail drooped and barely moved. Pushing himself closer to us, he raised his head with an expression of 'I'll be good'. The eye contact, and facial expression, along with the skillfully played reformed body language convinced us that he could adopt us. His energy level and acrobatic skills was evident when we asked him to get into the pickup truck.

We soon realized his skills far exceeded those shown us the first day. He immediately started us in an obedience program, to train us for his food selection, play activities, and the boundaries of his explorations. It was a tough sell, but soon food served was accepted, play consisted of fetch, and learning communication commands; not chewing ropes, water hoses, and saplings, into smaller sections. Chasing cats up trees was a no-no. Pre-chewing our garden vegetables for us was not an acceptable activity. Burying towels, shoes, boots, cooling cooking utensils, temporarily hung shirts and jackets, drying laundry, or anything else momentarily put down was also not acceptable.

Duke was immediately my wife's shadow and constant companion. He would protect her from strange noises coming from the woods, or visitors driving up the hill by jumping up and knocking Dolores down to the ground. After a two week period, I decided a test was in order. One shot was fired. A 22 cal. short makes very little noise. A whoosh was heard, and a vacuum was left in the wake of Duke's departure. Well, that's that. I enjoyed his company while he was here, and did not expect to see him again.

Later that evening he cautiously returned from out of the woods, his belly low to the ground, warily looking from side to side, as he slowly approached the back yard. He did not look happy to be back, but approached his feed pan carefully. Without a cowardly or embarrassed look, he delicately ate while surveying his surroundings. With loving restraint and reward, we finally rid him of his gun shyness. Soon, if a shot was fired and nothing fell for him to retrieve, I was reprimanded for my poor shooting ability with a gentle nip on the hand. I was still in his training mode.

When my son showed a reluctance to help me carry firewood, Duke would willingly pinch hit for him by carrying logs that almost matched his weight. BUT, he required payment. Every 3 to 5 pieces of firewood would have to be exchanged for a small piece of soft peppermint candy. For peppermint, he would carry wood all day long. During the peppermint lean periods, when wood was stacked, and the sweet tooth struck, he would go to the log pile, grab a medium size log, come to the backdoor and bang on it with the chunk of wood. Some mornings we could not open the door against the barricade of wood stack up against the outside of the door. An offering of a small stick to carry was insulting to him, and if a dog could scowl, his look was a scowl.

He also learned to climb trees by taking a running leap, scrambling up the trunk, and grabbing the lower limbs. Coming down, he never learned to do. His solution was to just fall to the ground. I was always anticipating broken bones. When leaning over a cistern opening, he would grab a pants leg or a shoe and hang on. If I was in a perceived dangerous position that he could not reach, his solution was to bark for help.

If I lay on the ground and acted like I was sleeping, he would settle down next to me and fall asleep. Sometimes, after he was asleep, I would get up and continue with my activities. When he woke by himself, he would show his disapproval of my dastardly deed by avoiding my eyes, keeping his eyes averted from me, or just plain ignoring my presence. In the evenings he would like to play hide and seek and soon learned to hide in the shadows, ready to pounce on me when I came close.

Duke's singing ability would make an opera singer take up a different occupation. He liked to accompany any style of music. Sirens were his favorite, but would readily join in and accompany humming, country, popular, or classic. He especially loved to show off his style of vibrato. He knew he was good, and if his singing was acknowledged and appreciated, his smile would dazzle you.

Duke would sulk if tied up. He demanded to be in the thick of all activity. He was not merely a dog, or a pet. He was a member of the family. He obeyed all commands, if told twice. "Duke, eat this," was a command he hated, because he knew it would taste bad. He was cunning and logical – if squirrel goes up a tree, squirrel has to come down. He would patiently wait at the bottom of an isolated tree waiting out the tree rodent.

He would not tolerate patronization. Chiding him with "whoosey little baby", or "poor little thing", or anything like that would bring out an air of indignation as though he was scratching grass and dirt at you with his hind feet. He never barked at strangers, only us when we were gone too long. With strangers he just smiled and showed them his extra long canine teeth. That was much more effective than barking. During his time with us he had been known to tree a few people without making a sound, his teeth, smile, penetrating eyes, and 120 pounds, a serious threat.

Duke allowed us to feed, wash, and sooth him for 17 years before old age and sickness took him away from us. His remains are by our house, where he loved to sit and watch, with a paw shaped stone inscribed with his name, date of birth and death. Often at night I feel his presence with us, his spirit guarding against intruders and night visitors.

The Museologist

Twist Stream, the Highland Museum Museologist, a person who restores, preserves and conserves museum artifacts, sat at his work bench, thinking back of his father Rip Tide Stream and his mother Flotsam. They had instilled the need to learn and understand the old ways in Twist.

Scrambled on the surface of his workstation lay a puzzle of old bones. He was ordered by that dumb museum director, Iam Smart, to get this pile of ancient calcium back into its original order. Hell, he did not even know what it is suppose to be. Those long pointed fangs should not be in a human skull and where the ligaments were originally attached to the bones, huge receivers were built up. Where in the human chronology was this thing situated?

Crap, it's 3:00 in the afternoon and I'll never get this done before my dinner date with Marylean Munrow. It took me three months to build up the courage to ask her out on a date, and even at that she thinks I had invited her out to talk about our upcoming project. It's hard for me to look across our workshop and see her in that mini-skirt and tight lab coat stretching across her...; stop thinking about her and get on with the work.

I'll just start with one bone at a time and not try to solve this reassembly all at once. Let's see, this goes to that, and that bone goes to this. Hell, this won't be as hard as I thought. Thigh bone attached to the knee bone, knee bone attached to the leg bone, leg bone attached to the foot bones. A little music in my brain should help me get done with this jig saw puzzle in no time at all. I might just get done in time to clean up before we meet at the Parkview Café in Marine. I wonder if she likes her hamburgers rare or well done; I bet rare. She strikes me as an adventurous type, one who chomps at the bit to take and finish new challenges. She really sinks her teeth into her endeavors.

Boy, this thing looks evil. I can't even begin to imagine what it looked like all fleshed out. Why in the world would a humanoid need fangs like that? It looked like something that belongs on a large cat, a lion or leopard, or something.

This museum is sure spooky when no one else was around. That rat-fink director ordering me to work on a Sunday takes the cake. Why his degree isn't even anywhere near what's needed to work in or run a museum. I think it is in English or Philosophy, or something like that. I should have his job; I'm trained to work in this environment. I can identify with all this stuff around me.

Well here goes that last bone. They all seem to fit. Well they should, since they all came out of that sealed lead coffin those excavators found in the salt marsh south of Marine. I don't think that salt production would be a very profitable venture for the Shaker Company.

Man, I can't keep my eyes open. And the smell from these deformed bones is fogging up my mind. Maybe if I take a real short cat nap I'll be fresh for my date with Marylean.

Before opening my eyes, I realize my neck hurts, and a bright light penetrates my eye lids. Oh, I left my work light on. What the hell just happened? I have to get up and move around a little. Where are all the bones? Their gone! What the hell is going on? I'll have to explain all this to that jerk director tomorrow.

I have to get out of here. I have a date with Marylean. I'll take care of all this tomorrow. I don't have time to clean up. I'll just make it to the Parkview.

Entering the café, I can see Marylean waiting for me. "Hi."

"Hi yourself," said Marylean. "You look different, older or something." Yes and definitely sexier, thought Marylean.

"Yah, it must be the long hours that Director Smart has me putting in. The strangest thing happened to me tonight. I finished assembling those bones out of that lead coffin, and they were gone when I woke from a short nap. It took me a while to get my bearings. But they were gone, all gone. Even the bone dust was gone."

"You'll figure it out. You're so intelligent Twist. Let's order, I'm so hungry I could eat anything put in front of me. You had better not sit too close to me Twist, I might even be dangerous."

"Yah, right," I replied. "But that situation back at the museum really has me perplexed. I just don't understand it. I closed my eyes for a few seconds, and when I opened them, the bones were all gone."

A slender waitress, with long legs, humming, "I'll be nice to you." took our order and returned shortly with two hamburger platters. "Twist, if you

50

want, we could go back to the museum after we eat, just to see if there is a rational reason for the missing bones. It's not too late you know." Laughing, she said "Maybe a dog snuck in and ate them."

"Eat your burger. Are you sure going back to the museum won't take too long? We could go to your place, just so we can talk."

Yes, I'll make you talk HUNK; I'll have you screaming your lungs out. You've never met anyone like me, thought Marylean.

Marylean did not click her seat belt on the way back to the museum. Her hot hand rested on my thigh. I have to force myself to concentrate on my driving. The traffic lights were a blur, but I knew her safety was in my hands alone.

Entering my lab puts a chill down my spine. I check the temperature, 75 degrees, so it must be me. I led Marylean down to my work station; where the bones were suppose to be. They were still gone. Marylean moved closer to me, her face an inch away, and she had a strange look on her face. I think she likes me! Her sweet cherry red lips came closer, parting, and I thought I could see long eye teeth that I never noticed before - just like in the missing skull.

"Relax Twist; it will all be over in a second. It won't hurt, you'll feel good, I promise," said Marylean.

Yah, now she thinks I'm a virgin, well she'll be surprised. I know a few twists and turns that might just impress her. I prepare myself, closing my eyes, gently pulling Marylean toward me. Tilting my head down, anticipating smooth, soft lips, I felt a gentle nip on my neck, then a penetrating sense of fear, as her teeth lock tight. Oh No! She is going to give me a hickee. Now how am I going to hide that, so high on my neck? What will everyone at work say? Everyone will laugh at me.

Ooooohh, what's that feeling coming over me from my toes? It must be love. I'll know when I look into her eyes. I just know we will be together forever. I'm getting faint just thinking about of a long future together. Pleasant dreams love.

My Ship Is Sinking

In the 1960's I was stationed aboard a naval vessel, a decrepit, leaky old Landing Ship Tank, U.S.S. Waldo County (LST-1163). It was a flat bottomed monstrosity that listed beyond the dangerous angle degree when encountering heavy seas. The decks were rusted through, it leaked like a sieve, and whenever we had a beach landing, the patches on its bottom were rubbed off. It was like riding a soaked sponge. Thoughts of a rescue replaced fears of sinking.

On one occasion, we lost the 1'x2' rubber seal that ran around the bow ramp, losing our water tight integrity. Water poured into the tank deck, a large cavernous space that took up over half of the ships length. The inrushing water carried cleaning rags, that the U.S. Marines used to wipe down their equipment, into the drains, and plugged the discharge pumps. Soon the tank deck was flooding. Our bow slowly settled down below the surface of the sea. We were in the midst of an angry Atlantic storm that battered us as we broached the wave swells, and accelerated our slide down to the watery troughs below. Eventually the forward two thirds of the ship was underwater, and we steamed backwards to prevent hydroplaning under the surface.

Volunteers were solicited to dive into the water of the tank deck, to dog down the equipment that was floating and bobbing about, bashing into the top decking and bulkheads. It was a very dangerous endeavor, but the sailors would get a shot of bourbon for each trip down. I did not volunteer. I restricted my soakings to the shower. Never a coward, I rather thought of myself as … prudent in my self preservation.

My wife was concerned, and the only information she could get was, "the ship was sinking." She could not understand why the whole squadron of ships; everyone but us of course, had returned to our home port, Naval Amphibious Base, Little Creek, Va. I guess everyone had faith in us, except us.

We eventually made our way through a Sargasso Sea to a rock shelf, in the middle of the Atlantic, where we could settle and open the bow ramp, at low tide, to drain out the water. Cleaning out the discharge pumps, and using our mattresses to seal the ramp, we managed to maintain an acceptable level of security against the rolling seas. When the incoming high tide floated our vessel, we set course for home.

We steamed slowly, to prevent losing our jury-rigged bow seal. It was somewhat uncomfortable sleeping on stretched canvas without mattresses, but considering the alternative, the crew was accepting of our situation.

It was always during ordeals such as this that I wondered why I join the Navy, and not the U. S. Air Force. Now, as I think back, reviewing my past, I realize that my past made my present.

Three Wishes

Three young lads, Clark, Travis, and Austin, were Trick-or-Treating in Highland, one early evening during Halloween. Taking a shortcut through the cemetery, each was trying to scare the other two with tales of horror. None of the three was successful in scaring the other two. Their pillow cases stuffed full of candies, fruit, and other delicacies, hung heavy in their clutching hands. They laughed at their future plight the next morning of stomach aches and feelings of sickness from the over indulgence this night.

A gentle sprinkling started to fall, with ominous clouds and the start of bellowing wind, warning them of downpours to come. Seeking shelter became their immediate objective. A concrete pavilion, built in the cemetery was the only safety they could find on such short notice. They sat huddled together for protection, as the wind howled, the rain poured, and the lightning created ominous shadows cast by the stones surrounding them.

There was no obvious memorial plaque or chiseled inscription dedicating a reason for the shelter. As the trio moved around under the roof to avoid the spray from the constant change in wind direction, Austin stumbled over a stone jutting up from the ground. Rain had washed away a thin layer of loose dirt covering the stone. Shadows from the lightning filled in the hollow lettering. "Under this roof, the three shall come. To right the fallen, for here is done. Lift the stone for three wishes sum. Their heart and mind, sell their souls to mine. For what they wish will solely bind."

Nervous laughter stuttered from the macho striving teenagers. "Yeah, right. I think we're granted wishes. One each," said Clark with a tight smile.

"Not me," said Austin.

"What a couple of wimps. Are we getting a little spooked?" stated Travis.

"O.K. smarty pants. What do you think it means?" responded Austin.

"I think we have to lift this stone so it's upright," said Travis.

The pillow cases full of sugary delicacies were set aside, as the three grunted raising the heavy stone. "Oh man, we got it upside down. Now we have to turn it over," moaned Travis.

More burst of released breathe, and ooohhs as the stone teetered off balanced, almost falling. Finally the stone sat upright, a gentle spray of rain washing rivulets of muddy water cascading down the surface, making an image out of a Bela Lougosi movie. Hair started to stick out and skin tingled when a flash of lightening knocked them to the ground. A smell of sulfur and sweet smoke filled the air. We checked ourselves, then each other, but could not find any damage, except for some smelly burnt hair. A smoldering flame drew our attention to the three burning pillow cases piled on the ground. The smell of burnt sugar dashed any thought of an evening feast.

A drenched old man approached in the rain, using a heavy looking cane in his right hand that sunk into the muddy ground with each step of his right foot. His face wrinkled much like a withered dried prune. He spoke with a voice that sounded like it was coming out of a long tunnel, like the subway that ran under Broadway. "You are each entitled to one wish, and you can see the results of your wish, before it becomes final. Your wish must be made within fifteen minutes. Speak out when you are ready."

Austin immediately shouted out, "I want a million dollars in gold."

Travis and Clark looked over to Austin to see a huge pile of gold ingots fall on him, crushing him to death. The scene cleared with Austin still standing there bug eyed, mouth standing open.

"No, no, I don't want that," he muttered.

Travis and Clark looked at each other. "I want to be a Lakers basketball star," requested Travis. A basketball rim appeared mounted on a backboard with a huge star with Travis's face on it. Big letters were printed above the star, "Lakers." "That's not what I want," stated Travis. The basketball net and backboard dissolved before their eyes.

The old man looked at Clark. "And you, what is your wish?"

Taking a full five minutes of thought, Clark finally spoke. "I want to be a hero."

A burial scene appeared before them. A minister was presiding over the coffin. "Clark was a hero, sacrificing his life to save another. The truck driver could not avoid hitting him when he pushed the toddler out of the way."

"No, I want to be a live hero," said Clark.

The old man disappeared in a cloud of smoke. The concrete pavilion and stone disappeared. The three youths stood staring up at the stars in the sky, their pillow cases of treats in hand.

"We're not telling anyone what just happened." They ran as fast as they could, each in a different direction to the safety of their homes.

A smiling drenched old man, with a face wrinkled like a withered dried prune, watched the three youths rapidly disappear from sight with a sinister laugh following them.

The Grave Opening

A number of years back when I was the Secretary-Treasurer and Sexton for the Marine Cemetery, I would have to call around to find available grave diggers.

I received a telephone call notifying me of a burial scheduled for Halloween. It was short notice, just two days away. I began working through my list. My calls proved to be non-fruitful, except for one possibility. He would call back the next day. I made myself available all day. At 5 p.m. I could wait no longer, and called hoping to hear a positive response. It was not my day, or rather not my night when I heard "No." Gathering my tools I prepared for a long night of work. A mantle lantern with spare mantles, two spades, shovel, grub hoe, grave template, ladder, canvas fly and plywood was assembled then packed into the back of my truck.

The evening was cool and the sky clear. A mild breeze kept the insects at bay. The sun was still up, enabling easy location of the grave site. Pumping up the lantern I gazed around the cemetery thinking of stories past; stories of graveyards and horror movies seen. Except for the wind sighing through the trees, the strange noises heard resembled moaning, or someone trying to softly talk to me. Other than that, everything was fairly quiet. The lantern seemed to become brighter, as the sun set over the horizon, and the cemetery became shrouded in darkness. I thought of the possibility of a passing county sheriff's deputy seeing a light, and stopping to check out the crazy guy digging in a cemetery on Halloween Eve.

Double checking for the correct grave site, I centered the template, and meticulously cut around its edge with my marking spade. The ground was solid and pushing the spade down six inches was laborious. The ground had not previously been disturbed. When the sod cutting encircled the template, the marker spade and template were placed back into the pickup. The digging spade pushed into the ground much easier than the marker spade. The sandy grit made a screeching sound as it scraped over the blade. I thought of fingernails scratching over a slate chalkboard, or frantic hands trying to dig their way out of a coffin. My senses told me that my mind exaggerated the sounds in my growing walled and ever deepening environment.

My mind became more active as the evening air cooled and became quieter. My senses began to pick up sound, smells, a heavier air weight, and a feeling of dread, as I slowly descended into the ground. Goose bumps appeared and I would glance around, with my eyes near level with the ground. Soon a ladder would be needed to get out of the hole I dug myself into.

Stories came to mind: setting up tape recorders to capture voices from the graves; using dousing methods to determine the sex and depth of bodies previously buried; becoming the possessed body of disturbed spirits with unfinished business. The deeper I dug, the more sinister the ideas become as they seeped up out of my mind.

Every time the spade encountered a root, or scratched past a rock, I would stop to look around, visualizing my best escape route out of the cemetery. The more mental focus put on the spiritual aspects, the less dirt was being removed from the grave site.

The ground fell away from the adjoining grave. Bits of rotted wood from the nearby coffin fell to my feet. The rolling soil sounded like words made from wind through a stand of trees, not coming from vocal cords. The loose granular dirt seemed to feel like weak hands fingering at the soles of my shoes as I shuffled to the other side of my hole. Taking a deep breath, I looked around while moving my lantern, trying to see into the shadows, trying to see if there was any movement. A cold sweat had broken from my brow to my toes.

Nothing was moving. Nothing was threatening. Nothing was out there, and nothing but me was in my hole. I continued to dig. Shove the spade down into the dirt, and throw it out on the pile. I would check my ladder; making sure is was still within reach. I could reach the bottom rung, slide it to the bottom, and scramble out in one fast and smooth motion. I thought I would be able to beat a world record, if there was one to be broken.

I felt a drop of moisture hit the top of my hat. Looking up I saw there were no clouds, no tree limbs or wire, or anything overhead. Not even night flying birds in the sky.

A shiver ran through my body as I chided myself for such foolish thoughts. Focusing my mind on the job at hand, I measured the depth, and began spading out the last layer. Half the ground was in my truck bed, and the backfill piled on the plywood and covered with the tarp.

Finally done, the tools were packed away, and the spirits assured I meant them no harm; I made my departure back into the realm of the living. What a way to loose weight and build up ones psyche. I made a mental note to remind the undertaker to try to give a more advance notification of future grave openings.

The Magical Switch

In my home on floor number two.

Sits my bed in a room with a view

And on the wall,

That's not so tall.

Sits a switch with a toggle of two.

A dark sucker switch, that's magical too.

If toggled down, the light soon drowns,

In a sea of darkness like Hades towns.

If toggled up, the light comes forth,

Sucking up darkness, with a worth.

Yes, a dark sucker switch,

Eating up the night, black as pitch.

It keeps the nightmares out of my mind.

It's surely God's greatest find.

The switch to stop my awful fright,

Fights the darkness with a might.

After a scary story,

Read on the second story.

And if by chance, the switch toggles down.

My head goes under my quilt of down.

Until my eyes, from under the covers I peek.

I find the light that I will seek.

In my prayers I say at night,

I ask my God to prevent my fright.

To keep my switch, always working.

So through the night, I am not worrying.

Salty

While stationed at the U.S. Naval Air Station Sangley Point, Philippines, with my wife Dolores and two children, son Lon and daughter Dee Ann, I heard stories from the local U.S. Coast Guardsmen about the wild cockatoo birds that live around the remote radar station at Zamboanga on the southern island of Mindanao.

One of the stories revolved around a Chief Petty Officer who was in charge of the smaller station. His constant companion was one of these birds. Other than himself, this bird was the only thing around that spoke English. During one of his trips back to Sangley Point, for a medical checkup, the local natives ate his cockatoo. The bird reportedly tastes like chicken, but then everyone says that just about everything, taste like chicken. The chief had spent many hours teaching his flying companion the English language. Upon hearing of the bird's demise, the chief became mentally unbalanced and refused to return to his station.

A small crew flew down to temporarily assume the unstable chief's duties. On their return, I was told of the tameness and ease of domesticating these wild relatives of the parrot. Since my command of seven U.S. Sailors provided the whole U.S. Coast Guard their complement of new stewards, it was relatively easy to talk them into bringing one of these flying critters up to me.

A week later, a local guardsman was knocking on my door with the ugliest thing I had ever seen cowering in a bamboo cage. Pin feathers sparsely covering its body and the bulging big eyes protruding from an exaggerated large head, locked on me and followed my every move. "Here's your bird Schwend, it must be about 10 days old."

"What the hell do I feed it? It looks like it should still be nursing or something," I said.

"That's your problem, I'm just the deliveryman," he replied.

Calling out, "Dolores, here's your bird."

"Oh my god, what do I feed it?" she said.

"I don't know, mash potatoes and milk, or maybe mashed bananas."

When I returned home for lunch, I asked Dolores how it went with the baby bird. "I tried both mashed potatoes and bananas. It ate some banana, but buries its head in the potatoes while it eats."

Lon and Dee came to the table to eat. "What should we call it?" I asked.

"Salty," shouted Dee. "It looks like it's covered with salt. Is it a boy or girl bird?" asked Dee.

"I don't know," I replied. "But I guess we will find out, sometime."

Salty soon became a member of the family. We found out she was a girl, but I don't remember how we found out. Salty began mimicking our words and feathered out. She was white, with a bright yellow crest, and bright orange under her tail feathers. It seemed she grew twelve inches overnight. She chewed on everything, tasted everything, and loved having the back and side of her head scratched. If one missed an itched spot, she would grab your finger and reposition it, squeezing until she was satisfied.

Her many unique traits surfaced over the first year. She liked to chase cats – she hated them. She would fight with a dog over a bone – she liked to break bones down into little pieces before she ate them. She was especially fond of barbequed pork chop and steak bones. She liked to portray a vulture, with head held down, wings out, and waiting for the kill command, at which time she would swoop down and attack a spinning jar lid, punching it full of holes, wadding it into a ball, and kicking it around on the floor. If Dolores turned on the vacuum cleaner, she would scoop the seed out of her feeder, onto the floor, just so there would be something to vacuum up.

Grass treats were usually taken to the top of her cage, dropped, and watched as the blades spun down to the floor. She knew she was the center of attraction, and if anyone received attention that she perceived was hers, they were immediately put into their place. Pecking order would be a fowl way of putting it.

Salty's cage was always open, except at night when covered, and she was sleeping. If the cage door was accidentally closed during the day, she would just make her own opening.

She knew how to open the cage door, but raised a ruckus when she dropped the sliding door on her toes if distracted. She was an early riser, but kept quiet, amusing herself, until the first sounds of family rising, when her entire jungle repertoire was vocalized, then you just knew Tarzan would swing in.

Salty saw me as her primary primate, coming to me first for attention. When young she would crawl inside my shirt, if open, and stick her head out to watch the world outside her house domain. She would often sit on my shoulder, nuzzling my ear, or cleaning my hair, one strand at a time. She never yanked a hair out, but once pierced my ear lobe while rough housing. She was shot out of the air with an accurate toss of a throw pillow.

She interacted with the whole family, playing tug of war with my son and his socks, and helping Dolores clean house. If she could not eat it, or enjoyed playing with it, it was destroyed. She was trained to use a trash can for her dumping ground, to save the furniture. Once in a while, maybe if the action was too urgent, she would use the outside of the can instead of the inside.

After returning to the mainland, we enjoyed many years with Salty. She developed a biological clock syndrome, I think. She started pulling her feathers out, and became irritable. Researching the symptoms, we discovered female cockatoos experienced this malady when not bred. There were no male cockatoos within a reasonable distance, so we had resorted to selling her to a breeder in Arkansas. We have never seen Salty again, but think of her often. Telling the many stories of our experience with her, to our friends, and sharing our photographs of her with them brings back happy memories.

Jungle POW Camp

Everything is black, as black as hell's womb. I can not stand up, and sitting on the floor made my knees buckle. The space is too short to stretch my legs out. Moans, groans, cursing, and men talking to themselves in a language that only they understand roll through this hell hole known as the Jungle Hilton.

A beam of light pierced the dark passageway between the tiger cages; small cells made of bamboo. A guard stopped at the primitive door to my personal torture chamber. He talks to me in bastardized English. "Tonight is Christmas Eve, American. What do you wish to receive tomorrow morning? We have water; electricity; leather straps; hot irons; or metal clubs for you to choose from. All you have to do is cooperate with us. Tell us the information we need and we will send you back home to your family. You do want to see your family again? Now, where are the other crew members? Where are they hiding? What was your mission? Give me the names of the crew."

"Screw you gook!" I spat through broken teeth. It sounded like I said, "sue yew hoot!" through my swollen bleeding lips.

My daily meal of watered down, wormy rice soup, is thrown through the bamboo bars into my cage. "Dumb Americans," taunts the retreating guard.

"Joe. Joe can you hear me?" I whisper. Joe has not answered me in the past twelve hours. I resigned to myself that Joe is dead. The last beating he took was bad. I don't think he ever regained consciousness. I return to whittling away at my prison with my sharpened belt buckle. Just two more lashings and I'll be able to crawl out. Then what? If I am caught, they will shoot me just to discourage others from escape attempts. That might be better than this torture.

Two hours has passed since the guard brought my slop. The lashings were cut. The bars slipped up through their supports and I should be able to squeeze through the opening. I had previously memorized the number of steps from my cell to the door when they dragged me to interrogations. The distance is impossible to convert to a crawling measurement. I'll just slide on my gut until I reach the door. I don't know if there is a wall around this compound. At this point I really don't care. I just want these monsters to know I'm smarter than they are.

Pushing, the door swings open, makes a sound like a silk dress falling off a pretty woman. A smile comes to me as I thought that I will remember that sound. Silently I crawl through, slowly close the door and crawl away from the guard's night fire. I wish I had a grenade, or something to stop their laughing. I visualized them hanging from the surrounding tree limbs. Another smile. They enjoy the pain and death they created with their torture.

I crawl through the jungle undergrowth, expecting a shot or bayonet in the back; or coming to a walled structure stopping my escape. Nothing! I stopped to rest; something grabs me, clamps my mouth shut and I hear, "Sssshhh. You're getting out of here sailor." I could make out the blacken face with two white eyes surveying the area. I pass out from the excitement. It was still dark when I came too. I feel the rotating motion of a helicopter in flight. I am scared to open my eyes, fearing my freedom was all a dream.

I panic as a loud buzzing alarm drowns out all other sounds. We're going down! We're going down! Fear screams through my brain. I open my eyes. Everything is black. I'm too scared to roll over, to realize that bamboo bars still surrounded me. Turning my head I see bright red numbers: 4:40 A.M. My hand slaps the alarm 'off' button.

My alarm clock blinks the changing seconds, reassurance, after a bad dream. I open the insulated bedroom drapes and see snow illuminated by the yard light. A deer slowly walks across the yard, stopping to nibble on a bush. I'm home, safe.

I think of those who did not come back and received a posthumous Purple Heart instead, a medal in exchange for their life. Then, I turn my thoughts toward my family and think how fortunate I am.

Merry Christmas.

The Hypnotist

Wanda sat at the kitchen table, her husband Clarence dribbles coffee from the cup held in his left hand while trying to pull a plate from the cabinet with his right.

"Why do you always have to be so messy?" She said.

"What? I want a piece of pie. I'll clean up my mess," he said with a disciplined puppy look.

"I would have to hire a full time maid to clean up after you, just to keep this place presentable. Damn, you're a mess," She replied with exasperation.

Observing Clarence go through his routine, she commented on his every move. "Close the drawer. Close the refrigerator door. Pick up those napkins you dropped on the floor. Put that dirty pie server in the dish washer. When you're done with your pie and coffee, you can pick up your dirty clothes in the bathroom and put them in the hamper. You can also turn off the lights in the bathroom, bedroom and pantry that you left on in the past fifteen minutes."

"Will you never let up? You're constantly on my case. I'll take care of it. Let me finish here."

Wanda reflected on her past ten years married to Clarence. He was a wonderful husband, if only he would pick up after himself. I have to follow him around like he was a six year old. I don't have a life of my own. Just following him around takes up all my time. I had to phone Babs to ask her husband Dave to call Clarence to go lawn mower shopping with him, just to get him out of the house and let me do some shopping, and relax for once.

Clarence was off with Dave and I finally got to the St. Clair Mall. Babs told me that a hypnotist was giving a demonstration this afternoon on 'Hypnotism can help you with everything.' Maybe a session with him would help me relax a little.

"People, hypnotism can help you loose weight, quit smoking, spruce up your love life, and correct bad habits," hawked the man standing behind the podium.

Wanda held up her hand and jumped to her feet, standing out in the crowd of fifty women, pulling their attention in her direction. "I have a slob of a husband. Can you correct that?" Laughter rippled over the gathering.

"Yes, see me after I'm done. I'll try to help you with your problem husband."

Sitting through the presentation, Wanda nervously waited for the last word, and maybe her salvation. Can he really help me? She thought. Ten women surrounded the speaker, the Fabulous McHenry. He was passing out business cards,

87

giving advice, telling the women to call to make an appointment. There were two big men, standing off to the side that looked like body guards. They began to herd the women away, escorting them toward the exit door. The Fabulous McHenry looked my way, nodded to me, motioning me up toward him with a wave of his hand.

"Now, do you want relief from your husband being a slob, or relief from letting it bother you?"

"Both," I said.

Handing me his business card, he said. "Meet me at my office in thirty minutes, 2:00 pm sharp. I have an empty slot from a rescheduled session, and I'll solve your problems." His smile was both confident and comforting.

"I'll be there."

I walked through his office door at exactly 2:00 pm. I was surprised to see one of the large men that previously accompanied McHenry, sitting at a reception desk.

"Wanda Bennett. Please go right in, Dr. McHenry is waiting for you."

"Oh, I didn't know he was a doctor."

"Oh yes, go right in."

Entering his office I saw a twenty by thirty foot room with partitions closing off an area that contained an examination table and other medical instruments. Two leather easy chairs sat at the front corners of his desk. Comfortable looking brown leather couch and arm chair sat next to the wall on his left. Impressive looking art decorated his office. Soft, relaxing music quietly wafted through the room.

Dr McHenry entered the room through a side door. "Ah, Mrs. Bennett, thank you for rushing here to be on time. I am truly sorry for the short notice, but this is the only opening for several weeks, and you sounded as though your need is immediate."

"Oh no. Thank you for seeing me so quick. I cannot tell you how grateful I am for this early appointment."

Softly he said. "Sit back on my couch, and we will discuss your problem, and the best way to resolve it. Good. Now just lean back and relax. Listen to the music. Listen to your favorite instrument. Keep listening, and now you will hear only the one instrument. Can you still hear my voice?"

"Yes."

"Now you only hear my voice, nothing else, just my voice. You will listen and obey my every command. And when you wake up you will follow all my commands from your subconscious, but you will not consciously remember anything from when you are asleep here and now. Do you understand?"

"Yess….."

I opened my eyes, looking at the ceiling tiles, with my head tilted, resting on the top of the couch back.

"How do you feel Mrs. Bennett?"

"Oh I feel wonderful, I feel ….. Well, refreshed and energetic. I haven't felt this good in months."

"Good, put your shoes on. You took them off to get more comfortable," said Dr. McHenry. Leaning over to slip on my flats, I noticed my skirt and blouse were not crisply ironed and a little wrinkled. I really should have ironed them better this morning before leaving home, I thought.

"Well, we have a solution to your problems. I have made an appointment for you to return in two weeks. At that time we will discuss the progress that you should see in your husband. You seemed tired and took a little nap. I am glad that you are now refreshed. While you were going in and out of your short sleep, we discussed your problems. Do you have any questions?"

"Questions, I don't remember anything. What...."

Dr. McHenry cut me off. "I think the music, being tired and rushing from the mall took a toll on your energy. You seemed very tired. But, as you said, you are very refreshed now. If you think of any questions before your return appointment, please call my office number there on my card. Thank you for coming, and make sure to take note of the changes in your husband over the next weeks. Yuri is at his desk and will call a taxi if needed."

"No. I'm parked down the block. I'm fine." I looked at my watch. 4:00 pm., could have I slept two hours? I must have been worn to a frazzle.

Getting home, Clarence was no where to be found. 4:45, I'll fix a pizza, pop a bottle of wine to let it breathe, and be ready for Clarence. What the hell was taking him so long to get home? He was supposed to be back at 4:00. At 7:P.M. I dialed Dave's number. "Hi Dave, its Wanda. Where's Clarence?"

"I dropped him off at 4:00 just like we planned."

"Well, he's not here. Where did he go, Dave?"

"I don't know. I saw him go up to your front door. He even bought a present for you. He mumbled to me that he made you mad this morning."

"I'll look for a note and check the back yard. Thanks. Bye."

I cradled the phone just as the front door opened. Clarence walked in with a dazed look on his face. He was holding a white plastic Wal-Mart bag in his hand.

"Here! I got you something."

Taking the bag, I took out and opened a blue box. A pair of green emerald ear rings sparkled up at me.

"I thought they would go with your green dress and that emerald necklace that you like so much."

"Well, thank you Hon. Their perfect. But, where have you been? Dave said he dropped you off three hours ago."

"I think I just got out of his car. Did he call you on his cell?"

"No, I just called him at home."

"Impossible," said Clarence. "O.K., O.K. I'll talk to Dave later and get this straightened out. I smell something wonderful that I bet my beautiful wife fixed for me."

Yah, right I thought. He's up to something. I'll give him enough rope to hang himself. He is not going to get away with this.

Clarence pulled the pizza from the oven, letting it sit on a baking stone to rest, and then poured the chilled wine before serving. He hovered over me, filling all my needs, like I was a princess. He acts the charming and perfect husband. Now I know he really did something bad. During dinner Clarence discussed all the things around the house I wanted done, and what would be needed with the yards to make them look better than our neighbor's yards. When I finished my meal, Clarence cleared the table, putting everything into the dish washer, wrapped the leftovers and put them in the refrigerator. He led me into the living room, turning on the TV and asked me what I wanted to watch tonight. What, no football? Whatever he did, it must have been a doosey.

I hear him fussing in the bedroom while I take my shower. Stepping out of the shower I see Clarence standing there with a towel in one hand, and my robe thrown over his shoulder. Taking off my shower cap, he gently dried it and then began to blot my body with the towel, started with my face and slowly worked his way down to my toes. He wasn't this attentive on our honeymoon. Then he helped me slip into the warmed robe. He must have held it under the heat lamp while I was showering. Walking into the bedroom was an eye opening shocker. The bed was turned down. The clean laundry from this morning was put away. The book I am currently reading was opened on my bed stand. I was fuming on the inside.

Forcing a smile, I said, "Thank you dear. How sweet of you. What have I done to deserve all this?"

"Nothing Love, I just thought you deserved a little attention since I was gone a while today. I hope you enjoy your book while I take my shower."

Slipping into bed, my mind was reeling with all the possible trouble he might have gotten into.

Clarence finished his shower and came to the bed wearing the favorite cologne that I gave him for his birthday. Getting into bed, Clarence gently touched me and gave me a kiss that knocked my socks off. Totally confused, I get out of bed with the excuse that I had forgotten to put some of my stuff away in the bathroom. The looks of the bathroom floored me. Everything was wiped dry, put away, and in its proper place. The room is immaculate! I soon forgot about reading the book, with all the sweet attention Clarence was giving me. My evening was exhilarating, something I never felt before. My sleep brought me dreams of fantasy.

Morning brings a bursting squeal of energy and excitement that overflows from the evening before. My body is full of enjoyment. Reaching over to caress Clarence, my hand finds nothing but warm covers. I hear music coming from the kitchen, smells of perking coffee and hot waffles fill the air. I throw on my robe and ran to the source of the mouth watering aromas. Freshly picked flowers rest in a vase at the center of the table. Orange juice, coffee, waffles, hot syrup and butter wait for my indulgence. Clarence reaches for my arm and guides me to the table, holding the chair to seat me. I must have died and gone to heaven, an old cliché, oh but how true.

Suddenly the plot is revealed to me. He has turned the table on me. Now I am the partner that was not holding up her part. He is not going to get away with that tactic. I'll just let him know that he is not treating me satisfactorily. The more he gives the more I'll tell him I need. He left for work with a kiss that would normally make me want to drag him back to bed. This wanton display of attention goes on for a week. Slowly I wear down. My mind and body can take no more. It was 10:00 a.m. and the doorbell rings. Filling the door opening was the monster mother of Clarence, my mother-in-law, my Nemesis, the Greek Goddess of vengeance.

She stepped into the room screaming "What are you doing to my son? I called him this morning to come over and mow my grass this evening, but he said no, because he is waiting on you hand and foot. Are you not capable of caring for your household without making a wimp of Clarence? That's no way to treat a man like my son. You had better get off your duff and treat him right or you will have to answer to me. Do you understand?"

"Yes mother Bennett. Clarence was just taking care of me because he thought I was a little peak-ed."

"Well there's nothing damn well peak-ed about you now. You had better shape up, or else!"

"Yes. Yes, please leave, your making me sick. Please leave." Shoving the old biddy backwards out the door, I heard, "Well I never...", as the door slammed shut.

Dr. McHenry was checking the computer screen, looking at his Cayman Island accounts, and finished laying out his investment portfolio strategy, as he started outlining more of the family genealogy charts, of the upper middle class families in town. The upper crust of society had lawyers checking every penny going in or out for them, but the middle strata of the community was much more lax with their monies.

Thinking of the hard times, a year back, when he was just released from the federal joint, he was pleased that he fell into this latest scam. There was plenty of time to learn and practice hypnotism with his captive audience in the pen. He cheated them of all their money. He had perfected every nuance in the applications of mind control. He could and did take everything he wanted from these pigeons. He has those two idiots, Yuri and Anton, set up for patsies in case anything goes wrong. Yes, he was eating pretty high on the hog.

Yuri buzzed the intercom announcing Wanda was here for her appointment. What an air head, but a good looking air head, he thought. "Bring her in Yuri," he said as he shut down his computer.

The door opened as Yuri said. "Step right in Mrs. Bennett."

Wanda entered into the room and walked up to the desk, sitting down in the big comfortable chair. "Good morning, Dr. McHenry."

"Good morning Wanda. You look in good spirits today." McHenry's eyes took in every aspect of Wanda. Yes, very good looking indeed, he thought.

Pushing a button on the inter-com, McHenry said, "Yuri, hold all calls while Mrs. Bennett is here. Now Wanda, I met and had a talk with your

Clarence, after your first visit. Why don't you sit on the couch, where you will be more relaxed? We will discuss your husband's current behavior."

"Sure" responded Wanda. Going to the couch, Wanda sat with her ankles off to the side and crossed. This music was perfect for relaxing, she thought to herself.

McHenry started to speak in his rhythmic soft voice. "Relax. Lean back and relax. Listen to the music. Listen to just one instrument. Now you can only hear my voice. You will listen and obey all my commands. When you awake, you will not consciously remember anything said while you slept. Do you understand?"

"Yeess...."

I opened my eyes. My head was leaning back on a leather cushion. My body was overly warm, and I felt an energy flow through my body. My mind was alert, telling me it wanted to do something to expend all the energy. I will have to jog or go to the gym this afternoon. I feel my face flush as I notice, like the last session, my skirt and blouse are wrinkled.

"You can get up now Wanda. Put on your shoes and we will set your next appointment. Are there any questions?"

"Not that I can think of right now," I replied.

"Good. I am very pleased with your husband's rapid progress. I think you will be happy with your family demeanor, from now on."

Oh yes, I thought. I love Clarence so much. He is the perfect husband. "Yuri will call you a taxi if needed."

"No, I drove here."

Driving home, Wanda thought of all the ways she could please her loving husband Clarence. Opening the front door, she called out to Clarence. "Honey, where are you. Are you home?"

"I'm in my study," shouted Clarence. Wanda found him deep in concentration at his computer.

"What are you doing Love?"

"Taking care of business, and where have you been?"

"Oh, just down at the mall looking for something to surprise you with."

"That's sweet," said Clarence tenderly.

McHenry, checking his e-mail, noticed one from wbennet@yahoo.net with a subject 'thanks from a happy patient.' Intrigued, McHenry opened the e-mail. A swirling image with mesmerizing coloration played on the monitor. A dreamy feminine voice starts talking, with a background of soft music. "Relax, listen to the music. Now listen to my voice. Visualize my every word. Relax. You want to sleep. Your eyes are getting heavy. Now your eyelids relax and close."

McHenry opened his eyes to a blank monitor. Quickly keying up his Cayman Island Account, he finds it empty. All funds were transferred to an unidentified account in Switzerland. No records of the transactions are recorded. "What is going on?"

Switching to his e-mail shows a blank listing and none in trash. "I'm wiped out".

He groans as he heard a loud banging with a shout, "Police, we're coming in." The door crashed in.

"What do you want?" A smiling McHenry smoothly said. It is always better to patronize the police, thought McHenry.

"You're charged with fraud and deceptive business practices, George Miller, alias Dr. McHenry."

Clarence sat at his computer, closed the anonymous e-mail to the Chief of Detectives, and quietly tallied up his new found fortune. Now I'll be able to quit my job as Head Engineer at Kyro Computers. Wanda entered his study. "Why don't we take a long vacation Love?" said Clarence.

Overweight Crewmember

It is hot, stinking hot. The humidity is drippy. The sun had turned the tarmac into a pressure cooker. If there is a hell on earth, this is it. The four Jig Dog (JD-1) aircraft (all the other services call it a B-26) are sitting in full sun; closed up, with the internal temperature 120 plus degrees.U.S. Naval Air Station Cubi Point is definitely not a summer resort. Even the scorpions are hiding from the sun. The birds are not flying. The flies are too hot to buzz or bite the back of your neck like they normally do. Sweat flows down the body and fills our rotten stinking flight boots. Bird droppings would have felt like a cool shower, if the birds had the energy to fly.

The flight crew strides out of the hanger to man their aircraft, eager to get aloft into the cool air at the 10,000 foot altitude. This is a four man crew, the pilot and one crewmember in the cockpit; the two remaining crewmembers manning the after station, behind the bomb bay. The cockpit is easily accessed through a single clam shell canopy. The pilot will have to crawl across the navigator's seat on the right to slide into his position. When flying with a five man crew, the fifth man sat on the deck, behind the navigator's seat, a jump seat with feet dangling in the bomb bay. The after station is accessed by jumping up and grabbing a metal bar, chinning yourself, swinging feet through a small open port. One of the after station crewmembers, Garcia, an ordnance man, is short and rather heavy set. He is supposed to pull the wheel chocks from the main wheels, and then access the after station.

Our squadron VU-5A has a complement of 45 men. We have to work hard to amuse ourselves, but watching Garcia is always a freebie. Sometimes we position a stool for Garcia to use, and sometimes we did not. We have the opinion that he needed the stool, not us, so he should be the one to manhandle the awkward thing. This time we failed to make the stool available.

We gather in the shade of the hanger, taking bets on how long Garcia would last before dropping out. Amazingly, he hung on, feet kicking, until the aircraft reached the turn up area at the beginning of the runway. There he let go and slumped to the pavement. The control tower traffic to the pilot was monitored by a radio in the hanger. Control Tower: "Jig Dog Pilot, you lost something out of your after station." Pilot: "Naw – just a fat crewmember." Control Tower: "Are you going to retrieve him?" Pilot: "Naw, let him walk back to the hanger. He can use the exercise." Control Tower: "Protocol calls for retrieval." Pilot: "Control Tower – this old beast is hemorrhoidal. We just dropped a fat one, how about clearance for take off?" Control Tower: "Jig Dog – You're cleared for take off."

Garcia must have lost a few pounds walking that long hot half mile back to the hanger. A victim of heat stroke could have accounted for his reddish, sweaty complexion and dragging body. His flight suit was opened and as he sat he fell into a coma like sleep. Burps and snores expel odors from the previous night's party.

Fun time being over, everyone goes back to work, with a few of us already planning the next day's adventure.

Lessons from a Goldfish Pond

Years ago my wife Dolores wanted a goldfish pond. After purchasing 6 feeder goldfish for ten cents each, we place them in a round stock watering tank nine foot wide and two feet deep, originally bought for a swimming pool when our two children were small. We enjoyed watching the goldfish dart around their new home, investigating all the nooks and crannies of the impromptu pool statuary placed there for both their pleasure and ours.

Some of our goldfish were black. The clerk who sold us the fish assured us that they would turn gold with age. Soon nuts in husks fell into the water from a nearby black walnut tree, staining the water a murky brownish-black. The gold goldfish were not easy to catch when we decided to move their watery home to a new location. We had to drain the tank in order to see the black goldfish. You would think they would be easier to catch as the water dropped, but they became more frantic in their evasive maneuvers. Finally, we had all the fish in a five-gallon bucket for their temporary lodging.

We purchased a large plastic storage container, with a twenty gallon capacity, to hold the fish over the winter. We placed the fish in the tank on a stand next to a double set of south facing windows. During the winter months we noticed the fish always gathered at the east end of the tank in the evening. We finally realized that they were watching the television with us in the evening. If we came into the room to sit, they would come to the side of the tank nearest to us. They were always hungry. We were always adding water to the tank which would make a non-analytical person think they were drinking too much, but we concluded that evaporation was the culprit.

In the spring, I dug a large deep hole on a grade sloping away from the east side of the house, in view of our living room bay windows. Landscaping around the pool with flowers and green plants from the surrounding woods made a cool and relaxing retreat. We added a waterfall made of large giant sea-clam shells and on the opposite side, paved a semi circle with stepping stones. The fish were happy, jumping out of the water, splashing, and darting around.

It wasn't long before we noticed baby fish swimming around. We must be doing something right, or rather; the fish were doing something right. The gold fish grew and grew, their tails becoming long and fancy. Some tails were longer then their bodies. Eventually some of those one inch fish grew to be fifteen inches long.

Now it's been read that gold fish have a thirty second memory, but they remember that they are going to be fed, or think they should be fed, whenever they see us walk to the edge of the pool. They gather at the surface of the water making smacking noises with their mouths and splash water with their tails. That must be a form of sign language saying "feed me, we're hungry." If you put a hand in the water, they will come to your finger and nibble or kiss. I wonder if they are thinking that they are kissing the hand that feeds them. Whenever I get in the water to clean out debris, or retrieve a fallen stone, they will bite and pull the hairs on my legs. Are they hungry and think they're feeding on my leg hairs, or, are they trying to remove an imaginary parasite from my body, keeping me in good health? It doesn't matter what they're thinking, it tickles.

My grandchildren were visiting and I told them to go out and feed the fish. I said, "Whistle as if calling a dog when you walk up to the pool. I'm training the fish to come when I whistle." Sure enough, Travis whistled. "Grandpa," he said, "It works; the fish came when I whistled." Now, am I training the fish, or, are the fish training me, or, are my grandchildren patronizing an old fool, or, are the fish fooling everyone to get more food?

I think my fish are spoiled. They expect to be fed manufactured fish food. If I throw a bug into the water, they ignore it. I move potted plants around in the water, and they push it off its stand. I turn off the waterfall where they like to play in the turbulence, or turn off the air bubbler where they like to float and get a bubble massage; they will retaliate and hide under the foliage. Can they rationalize cause and effect? Are they punishing me by hiding?

If the fish are not fed to their satisfaction, they will destroy the plants, pulling them out by the roots, letting them float on the water surface, and finally eat them like the little monsters they are. I would put the water plant instructions into the water for them to read, but I think they would stick their gills up into the upper strata of their world, and not read how luxurious, and fast spreading the plants are, and how their presence benefit them by filtering the water and introduce oxygen into their little stuck-up world.

I am now trying to formulate a plan to correct this watery neighborhood problem, and I will keep you advised on how it is going.

Joe

I had been in the Philippines a month and already realized that a different country would have suited me better. Acclimation to the heat and humidity still evaded me.

Sitting at an outdoor restaurant in Olongapo City, drinking a San Miguel beer, I was feeling sorry for myself for being in this sodden country, while waiting for my meal.

Taking in the street sights, my eyes focused on a little man, shorter than four foot tall walking toward me, along the dusty path. He was muscular and had black kinky hair. As he came closer I noticed his yellow gnarled teeth, and that his dark yellow eyes were streaked with prominent red blood veins. His gait and bearing showed pride and an air of superiority.

The little man's eyes focused on me as he became aware of my staring. His direction of travel changed a little, to center on me. When he was about ten feet away from me, I raised my hand to acknowledge him. He hesitated, and then came closer, about five feet closer. I had dropped my hand, thinking that I may have made a mistake. He might be thinking I thought I knew him. We looked at each other for a few seconds. He was sizing me up. Quickly I introduced myself, "Hi, I'm Chuck Schwend", gestured toward an empty chair, and said, "Let me buy you a beer."

Without responding to my offer, he said, "Do you know who I am?"

Laughing, I answered, "No, but I'll still buy you that beer." The small man studied me for a few seconds, and then sat.

The waiter approached without my meal. He was nervous and stood behind the little man sitting across the table from me. "Is he bothering you, sir? Would you like for me to call the police?" The little man did not move or change his facial expression.

"No," I said. Looking across the table I asked my new acquaintance, "Would you like something to eat?"

He shook his head indicating, "No."

Looking at the waiter I said, "Bring a beer for my guest." The waiter's face scrunched up in disapproval, then left without saying anything.

A smile was on the small man's face, and he said "My name is Chief ??????????" stating a name that neither my tongue could get around nor my mind comprehend.

I told him, "I'll never be able to pronounce that."

"Then call me Chief, or Joe if no one is around." The waiter approached with the ordered beer, quickly setting it down while turning to leave.

"Bring another for each of us," I said. The waiter grunted and nodded his head while walking away.

Joe stared at me and said, "You are different than most men."

"I was going to say the same to you," I replied. We both laughed politely. "You know that they don't like Negritoes sitting here?"

"Well", I said, "Maybe they don't like me here either." Again, we both laughed.

The waiter approached again with two more beers and my order of fried rice. Without speaking, he set the meal down on the table and left. Joe watched me eat while drinking his beer. He did not attempt to interrupt my meal by speaking to me. When I was done, he drank his beer slowly, swallowing his last as I was finishing mine.

Still smiling, Joe spoke slowly, "I am Chief of the Seven Zambales Pygmy Tribes, and I would like for you to visit me at my village. Tell any Jeepney (a local taxi made from a jeep) driver, they all know where it is. Come this weekend. I will be expecting you."

"Sure," I said. "I'll be there." This was the beginning of my friendship with Joe, the Chief.

The Jeepney driver was reluctant to take me close to the pygmy village entrance. He dropped me off about 100 yards out. The land was cleared and grassless around the village, with few trees growing inside the perimeter. The sun felt like a close heat lamp in a sauna, beating down and baking exposed flesh.

Small people were conducting their everyday activities, and none gave me more than a fleeting glance. Stopping a woman, bare to the waist, nursing two small babies, I asked, "Where is the Chief?"

Transferring one baby to her shoulder, she used her free hand to point to the largest in a circle of nepa huts. As I came near to the grass covered residence, the chief stepped down a five foot ladder from the doorway. He greeted me, and invited me to rest in the coolness below his hut. A woman splashed water onto a hanging sheet, to cool the air with evaporation. All the short women were bare to the waist, but this woman was taller, and did not resemble the other people I could see. She looked like a deeply tanned girl that could have come from the states.

Joe noticed my interest and said. "We hid many Americans during the war. Their presence brought new blood to my tribe. We have benefited and prospered." And with a gleam in his eyes, said. "And we are always looking for new blood."

Following that first visit to the village, I always brought a case of San Miguel beer when visiting. On one visit, I was wearing shorts. Joe noticed a dermatitis problem that the Navy doctors were trying to clear up. They would prescribe a tube of medication with "Try this and see how it works." This happened more times than I was happy with.

"That is not good," declared Joe. He summoned his personal physician to examine me. The short witch doctor carefully examined my legs, mumbling something I could not understand. He left for a while, returning with roots and other vegetation I could not identify. Grinding everything into a poultice, he slathered it over my legs. Joe interpreted his instructions, mainly being, 'do not wipe or wash it off'. The next morning, the red and black blisters were gone, along with my suntan.

Returning to the base, I went to the sickbay, showing them the witch doctors results. They took a sample from the little of the smeary mess still sticking to my legs. "We'll send this in for analysis." They did not like me calling them a bunch of quacks.

I enjoyed many visits with Joe during my tour of duty. Many years later, I did return to the

Philippines, but I never saw Joe again. However, I did make him a prominent character in my novel "Dragon Dreams".

Dowser

Dowsers are a unique group of individuals. The most common is the Water Dowser, a person who can find water, tell you how deep the vein is in the ground, how wide the vein, and in which direction the water is flowing. The best usually will not tell you their secrets. The wannabes and the amateur blowhards will delight you with their mighty tales of flowing finds.

The successful dowser will normally use materials they are most comfortable with. Some use tree or brush forks. Some dip the forks in water just before using, and some just use dry forks. Other successful dowsers will use metal legs, wire, or even welding rods. Long or short instruments, or what ever the person uses, he will swear is the best. Personally, I prefer long bare 10 gauge copper wire resting in two short pieces of copper tubing held in my hands. The tubes allow the wires to swing easily, making them more sensitive, to read the water.

Most people with a positive electrical system in their bodies will show their instruments crossing in front of them when centering above a water stream. When the instruments swing outward, to hit the outside of the arm, it shows people with a negative system. Some of the people with a negative system have medical problems that are quite visible, and I don't ask the others that look healthy. I guess their yin/yang is messed up, and I do not know who they should see to get it fixed. It's their problem and up to them to get cured or corrected. I'm sure they would become upset or angry with me if I would mention my suspicions to them.

To establish where the water veins are located under a section of ground, the dowser will walk a grid, placing markers where ever water is found, to map the veins. The area where the most veins cross will be investigated to determine depth and quantity of water available. If this spot is not desirable due to its location, the area where the second most veins cross is investigated, and so on. This cross vein feature is desirable due to the possibility of a vein drying up, leaving the other veins to compensate. Any vein less than 15 feet is discounted because it may be a high water table vein, which could dry up when the water table drops.

I will not tell you the secrets of how the dowser determines the vein depths and widths, or how he determines the direction of the water flow. It is superstitious on my part, but I feel I could lose my gift to read the signs I see and feel.

It is also possible to find old water lines, sewer lines, and old springs that went back underground. It is not possible to find standing non-flowing water, like an old well location, but the veins leading to the well are findable.

I have never failed to prove that dowsing works. Some claim that water is everywhere, and all that is needed is a well digger. Well, anyone who has paid for dry wells can attest to the error of that vein of thought.

I have never charged for my services, but have accepted gas money. Occasionally, small amounts of money finds it way to the seat of my car or truck, or have been bought a meal, but I have never been given a chicken, eggs, a ham, etc., as others have claimed they received.

Some dowsers claim they can find gold, silver, and oil. I have never met any of these claimers, but have read about them. Note that I have never read of a 'verified' finding. I feel they are in the realm of palm or card readers. Other dowsers claim that they can determine the depth of a grave, and the sex of a body buried. I know the procedure but have never tried it, but then no one has ever asked me to perform that service for them.

I think I'll try dowsing for silver or gold. Who knows, I might get lucky and rich. I understand that there is an old lost silver mine north of Highland. Legend has it that Silver Creek was named after the mine.

I don't think talking about the possible mine location would be healthy for me. People would think I am strange if I were to be seen walking around their property with my arms stuck out in front of me. Also, anyone who thought they knew me might just start following me around. That would make me nervous, and my neck would get stiff from looking back over my shoulder.

After reviewing everything written above, I guess that sticking with water dowsing is the healthiest direction to go. No one would get angry at me, or suspicious of me, and I would get a good feeling from knowing that I was helping others, in need of a good water source.

A Sailor in Japan

It was a cold, wet, November night in 1956. I had just reported in to my new command, VP-9, at Iwakuni, Japan, an old Kamikaze base during WWII. The personnel of my new squadron occupied the vintage barracks left over from the war. The area around Iwakuni oozed with interest, with its ancient history and standing structures dating to the sixteenth century.

The members of the command had invited me to join them at one of the local watering holes, but I felt my interest was more to seeing the local culture.

After finding my way to the older part of the city, a business district of sorts, a lit sign with food displayed on it beckoned to me. An off-limits card stuck on the entrance door momentarily stopped me.

A nervous maitre d' approached me, pointing to the card on the door. Ignoring his gestures, I walked in and pointed to an empty table. Another employee rushed up and spoke to me in English. "Sir. You cannot come in, this is off-limits."

"I won't cause any trouble," I said. A growling low pitched comment came from an elderly man in traditional Japanese clothing, sitting at a small table with a younger woman, off to the side of the dining room. From his speech and the look on his face, I could tell he did not like me being there. "A bowl of soup and a bottle of Asahi beer is all I want," I said.

The maitre d' said "dami, dami (bad, bad)."

The waiter spoke to me, "Here, sit by the door and I will get your order."

The glowering stare from the old man was making me feel uneasy. It seemed everyone in the restaurant was looking back and forth from me to him. The waiter returned with a hot bowl of noodle soup and beer. "Send a drink over to the old man," I said.

The waiter nervously glanced over to him and said, "Yes, but do not attempt to talk to him. Do not look at him."

I studied the old man from the corner of my eye whenever he was not looking my way. He was tall for Japanese, and the young woman sitting with him was very attractive. She was sitting at the table facing in my direction.

The waiter arrived at his table with sake wine, causing an outburst of apparent cursing, or at least it sounded like cursing. He dismissed the waiter with a wave of his hand, and gestured toward me while talking with the woman at the table.

The soup was delicious, and the beer hit the spot. After paying my bill, I left thinking I'll have to remember how to get back here.

One week later, I returned to the restaurant. When the waiter saw me come thru the door, he gave me a look as if to say, oh no not again. Looking over, I saw the old man and the woman sitting at the same table as before. I was seated, and ordered a rice and vegetable meal with green tea. Glancing over to the old man, I told the waiter to take a drink over to him, just like before. This exchange of looks, drinks, and non-understood comments continued weekly for over a month.

Entering the establishment, I was seated and ordered my meal. The waiter came back and asked if I would follow him over to the old man's table. I was left standing by the table, with no chair to sit on, as the old man said, "I am Onan Kikkawa. This is my great granddaughter. You will not look at her. You will not talk to her. You will not acknowledge her." The waiter hesitantly brought a chair for me,

132

and then brought my meal. I did not know if I should eat in the old man's presence or not. After a few minutes I clumsily tried to get food to my mouth, while not looking at my bowl, but with eyes locked onto his.

"All Americans are barbarians. They have no honor. They are loyal to no one. They have no respect. What response do you have to that?" He said.

"Yes," I said. "I know a few like that."

"I will tolerate your presence at my table," he said, "but only if you respect my country and me. Do you think you can do that?"

"Sure," I replied. "Where did you learn to speak English so well?"

"I studied in England, years ago," he replied.

We met nearly every week at the restaurant. The young woman's name was Minkoto, but she was not always with him. What he did not know was Minkoto and I met in secret. She had a very restrictive life but was fascinated with the American culture. She wanted to know everything about America and its customs.

One evening Onan Kikkawa told me he was samurai, dropped his kimono off the shoulder, proudly revealing his large dragon tattoo.

"Drunken sailors get tattoos like that all the time," I said.

"Barbarians, all Americans are barbarians," he said, slamming his cane down on the table, knocking tableware to the floor. He looked at the smile on my face and said, "You should not take me so lightly," and then he too smiled.

In the spring of 1957 Minkoto was killed by the Yakusa, and I have never seen or heard from Onan Kikkawa since.

The Dishwasher

Brit Speres stood at her dishwashing station in the Parkview Café. Her long legs plunging down out of her short shorts, covered with a rubber apron that protected her from the steaming hot water. The hot damp air caused her dark cascading hair to curl around her face and neck. She preferred the hectic pace of scraping, rinsing, washing and then rinsing again, trying to keep up to the demand for clean tableware, to the table hopping duties of a waitress. Brit did not care for the narrow space between tables, where she was forced to bump against, and slide past the hungry patrons in the dining areas.

New clientele soon learn not to try becoming overly familiar with suggestive ambiguous language during or after ordering food and drink. Brit's feet at the bottom of her shapely long legs would become deadly and accurate when used as weapons. The rough customers did not find it encouraging when they found themselves flat on their back, looking up at a beautiful but hardened combatant face. The smooth Casanovas were whittled down to wimp level with Brit's belittling retort to the come-on lines they thought so beguiling.

Once in while Brit would sub for the cook, especially when she knew that Jack was coming in for a late breakfast. Jack, from a wealthy family, had a roving eye, and was a big tipper. Brit remembered Jack's standard order; oatmeal with bacon and tomato on toast. She always tried to sprinkle his oatmeal with her grandmother's secret love potion; a supplement she knew would eventually bring him to her arms. A firm believer that food is the way to a man's heart, she followed her great grandmother Tillie's advice on how to trap and keep a man. Tillie always said that men were like dogs, that they would lick the hand that fed them what they liked, and Jack's oatmeal, bacon and tomato on toast is always the best available, and to his liking.

Brit could not indulge in her favorite pastime, daydreaming about her future, while cooking. Occasionally she would slip into a stupor, dreaming of life with Jack, while the grill would get hotter, burning all the food. Focus, I have to stay focused she thought. When she was washing dishes, her flushed face was always attributed to the steam that would engulfed her face, and no one would believe her fantasies was the culprit.

"Someday, yes someday, Jack will be mine," murmured Brit to herself. I know my plans are working. Jack never failed to say hello to the workers in the kitchen. His smile made the waitresses hearts flutter, and their minds fluster.

He was a big tipper, but his smile would be enough to satisfy any one of them. Yes, he is my prize, Brit thought.

Jennifer hesitated while taking an order back to Kathy the cook. "Jack just came in with a sizzling hot babe. You'll have to peek out and check them out," she said giving Brit a smug smile.

Dropping the plates into the sink splashed the water up and over Brit's head, her soaked hair sparkled with little dish detergent bubbles sticking out like ornaments on a Christmas tree. Brit growled to Jennifer, "let me take their order so I can get a real close look at that tramp." Throwing the rubber apron to the side, Brit stopped to compose herself, and then ambled out with order book and pen like weapons at ready.

She spotted them in the corner, heads inclined toward one another like they were scheming an elicit love affair. Striding toward the pair, Brit noticed that the stunning young woman, a beautiful blonde, blue eyed goddess that any Miss America would be jealous of, was hanging on every word out of Jack's Adonis mouth.

Stopping at the table to take their order, the woman looked up and choked trying to swallow down a laugh. I remembered that my hair looked like I shampooed and stepped out of the shower without rinsing. I felt my face flush. Jack looked at me with a smile that told me he was laughing with me and not at me. "Hi Brit, this is Jeanne, and Jeanne, this is Brit, the best cook, waitress and dishwasher in the area."

Brit locked eyes with Jeanne, visualizing Methuselah, snakes for hair, gnarled teeth, and breasts that hung to her knees, then said ever so sweet, "so nice to meet you, have you known Jack Long?"

"Oh yes, from our earliest childhood. We have always been very close," Jeanne replied.

Brit's body was rigid with the urge to extend her nails to claw out those big blue eyes. "That's nice. What can I get you two to drink, and do you know what you want to eat?"

"Ice tea and yes," Jack said flashing his bedroom eyes, "we'll have the special."

Brit turned smartly, taking the order back to Kathy. Brit did not like to mumble, she thought it made her look weak, a trait she did not like. Today was an exception. The thoughts just spilled out of her mouth, babbling in non-decipherable nonsense. "Here, throw some slop on a plate for that gold digger sitting out there with Jack."

Kathy returned the dig with a knowing smile, "a little up tight are we? What are they ordering? Hey Brit, the slip is blank. Come on, get your act together."

"Oh, they just want the special. Just throw something on a couple of plates and I'll take it out to them," Brit said.

"You are not going to get tender feelings from Jack treating him like that," said Kathy. "Get back to those dishes, and I'll let you know when their order is ready."

When Kathy set the plates on the ready counter, Brit still fuming picked up the order for Jack and 'that hussy'. Approaching the table, Brit was thinking how well the food would look decorating Jeanne's hair. A broad smile remained on her face with that thought, as she set the plates down on the table.

"Where's our tea?" asked Jack.

"I'm sorry. We are so busy today. I don't know if we will ever get caught up," stammered Brit.

Jack did not reply but looked around at all the empty tables. "Oh yes, Sis could also use some sugar. She likes her tea sweet," said Jack.

"Sis?" Brit said slow and questioning.

"Yes, Jeanne is my sister, out to visit me for a couple of weeks. She just graduated from SCLU with a Masters in Business. She's looking for a job. Do you know of any openings in the area?"

"Now how in the world would I know anything like that?" Brit answered.

Jack just smiled as Brit left. Returning to her sink and dirty dishes, she remembered the two ice teas. "Damn!" Now her face was really flushed. She had to go back out there, humiliated, like she did not have a brain in her head. She set the two drinks on the table, and turned around to go back to washing dishes.

"Jennifer, tell me when Jack and his sister need refills. I have to get him to ask me out on a date. Once I have him to myself, he'll be putty in my hands. After a few dates with me, he'll be begging to put a nice big diamond ring on my finger. He won't be able think of anything else but me," Brit said in a dreamy voice.

"Sure thing Brit," said Jennifer, thinking that Brit was the most brazen gold digger she has ever heard of. She should not even be allowed in the dining area with those highly suggestive hooker aides she calls clothes. A few minutes later, Jennifer rounded the corner saying, "O.K. Brit, you're on."

Giving herself a check in the small mirror on her wall, she frowned. Pushing her hair in place, she threw her apron on the counter; smoothed her tight blouse; attempted to pull her shorts down to a presentable level; adjusted her bra; and pulled her shoulders back while putting the most come hither smile she could on her face.

The swing of Brit's hips could have churned butter as she approached Jack's table. "How about some refills?" coo-ed Brit.

"Sure," said Jack.

As Brit tilted the pitcher to pour, Jack lifted his glass toward Brit. The iced tea poured over the table, flooding the surface, and ran down onto their laps. Jack and Jeanne immediately reacted by jumping to their feet, and overturned the table that fell on Brit's big toe. Brit uttered a loud cat killing scream. She raised her foot in the air, and then fell backwards onto another table with uncapped mustard and ketchup bottles that Jennifer was filling. The table collapsed and Brit ended up sitting on the floor crying, covered with mustard and ketchup. Jennifer thought the effect was becoming, and was a true upcoming for Brit. Brit sat on the floor crying, and just knowing that her life was ruined. Jack would never think of going out with a klutz sitting on a floor covered with condiments.

Jack, being a true gentleman, did not try to wipe away the tea soaking into his clothes, but immediately went to Brit's aid. Bending over to pull Brit to her feet, he did not realize that her struggling was due to her embarrassment. Brit, in her attempt to push away from Jack, to remove herself from the situation, slipped in the slippery mixture on the floor. Her feet pushed Jack's legs out from under him. Jack released his grip on Brit's arms and tried to maintain his balance. Brit fell back to the floor with a hollow thud. Jack who is now horizontal in the air over Brit fell toward the writhing body below him.

Brit yelled, "Oh no."

Jack yelled, "Oh no."

Jeanne yelled, "Oh no."

Jennifer yelled, "Oh crap."

Kathy yelled, "I don't believe this."

Dunwyn, sitting at a corner table said, "This is the best damn slapstick comedy I have ever seen. I'm eating here more often."

Brit, tried to catch her breath and looked up at Jack gasping for air, "Get off me you big lout," rolled him off with a practiced push and shift of her body.

Jeanne, maintaining her footing, helped Jack to his feet.

Brit struggled up, feet slipping in the muck. She made it to the restroom, to make herself presentable, and locked the door. Jennifer came pushing a mop bucket for a clean up.

In the unisex restroom, Brit splashed cool water onto her face, looked in the mirror saw red puffy eyes. Pulling out several paper towels, Brit continued to cry. She blotted her face and sat down on the toilet. Loosing her balance, she slipped down into the water. "Crap, some idiot guy used the toilet and didn't put the seat down." Jumping to her feet she looks down and realizes what just happened.

A screeching scream of ten dieting women, who just found out that the watercress sandwich they just consumed, contained 30,000 calories, punched through out through the restaurant. Everyone in the eatery froze, thinking a macabre murder was taking place, waiting to witness the escaping villain. Jack, hearing Brit's scream, dropped the towels he was using to wipe away the catsup and mustard, ran to the restroom breaking in the locked door. Brit was leaning against the door, trying to figure out why her life ended like this. She was propelled across the tiny space, hitting her head on the facing wall next to the mirror. She slowly crumbled to the not so clean floor, and lay unconscious. Jack pushed hard to open the door wide enough to squeeze through. Jack carried Brit's limp body out of the restroom to the back dining area, confirming everyone's suspicion that someone was actually murdered, and from the soaked condition of the victim, assumed death was from drowning.

While unconscious, Brit dreams of life with Jack. Her life has turned around and is happily married to Jack. Her materialistic passions no longer drove her. She was in bed with Jack, moaning. Jack heard the moans and thought she was deep in pain. As Brit wakes she opens her eyes, seeing Jack leaning over her, his face just inches from hers. Reaching up she pulled Jack's face down, kissing him passionately. Jack responds.

Two years later, Brit is in her kitchen preparing breakfast. Jack enters and embraces Brit as she stands in front of the stove, flipping the eggs and patties of sausage. He nuzzles her neck, and said, "Good morning love", then walked to the table where he wiped the chin of little Jackie, sitting in her high chair eating oatmeal.

My First Bee Colony

My wife Dolores discovered a bee swarm balled on a pine tree growing in the front yard. The swarm was huge, a living pulsating threat, larger than a basketball. The banded insects were excited, flitting around, waiting for the scouts to return with the news; the location of their new home.

We quickly studied the situation. A hive brood box was required. A trip to my neighbor filled the need for equipment and advice. Holding the tip of the limb supporting that fluid looking mass of potential trouble firmly in my hand, I snapped the slender appendage like a leather whip. Bees dropped like dead weight, falling into the brood box positioned directly below them. Spraying sugar water onto the buzzing, boiling heap subdued them as they cleansed themselves before exploring the new domicile presented to them. Organizing themselves, they went to work cleaning the drawn foundation positioned in wooden frames for them. The Queen's maidens busied themselves attending to the matriarch of the hive.

Ensuring all the bees were hived in the box, I carefully set an inner cover over the box, followed by a telescoping weatherproof lid. Their murmurings told me that they were content. Gently lifting the hive assembly, we carried my prize to their permanent location. Thoughts of the taste of delicious honey were already watering our mouths.

While educating ourselves on our new charges, we read that bees will come to an adopted beekeeper for help if they find themselves in trouble. We had a good chuckle that led to laughing to what if situations. Months later while inspecting our fruit trees, a lone bee came to us, flying in vertical circles, right in front of our faces. At first we thought we were being warned away, as bees would normally slap you before stinging, but she would fly back toward the hive after making a few circles, then return and repeat her aerobatics. Curious, we approached the hive and saw wasps were attacking the workers as they left the hive, and then apparently took the paralyzed bees back to their nest to feed larvae. A strong straight stick, and a lack of common sense, allowed us to dispatch the invaders. Our bees hummed their approval.

A month later we were rewarded with several gallons of clear honey to sweeten our tea, toast, and bread. We had rediscovered an ancient cooperative between insects and man, but, have not decided who is smarter, the bees or us, as we have to adapt ourselves to the will of the bees.

Return to the USA

It was July, 1960. I landed in California after leaving a jungle in the Far East, via Taiwan and the Red China Mainland. Just turning 21, I had high expectations for my first sight of the United States in two years. The Vietnam War was in full steam. The air seemed to have a different smell and flavor than what I remembered. The street sounds had a different tempo. People were nervous and acted apprehensive, almost paranoid. Then I noticed the insane-acting group throwing eggs and spitting on the uniformed service members.

I watched them from inside the gate. They flaunted red and green colored hair, hissing, snarling, and barking like animals overdosed on Dexedrine. The guard noticed my reluctance. "You'll be alright," he said.

Easing through the gate with my sea bag and an overnight bag in hand, I heard shouts of "Baby Killer; Murderer; Rapist;" and worst of all, "Coward."

Quickly, I flagged down a taxi. Ducking flying debris I slammed the door shut. The driver looked back over his seat and said, "You're a brave sailor walking out that gate into that group of trash."

"What the hell is going on?" I asked as he drove down the street, avoiding the people demonstrating on the pavement.

"Nuts protesting the war. Sometimes they throw red paint or blood on you returning servicemen. Now-a-days, you never admit you're a veteran. Hard telling what could happen to you. Where are you going?" he said.

"I don't know. How about out to a main road where I can hitch a ride back to Illinois."

"You had better not. It would be a lot safer for you if I took you to the bus station. You could change out of that uniform and get your thumb air worn, starting in the next state."

"O.K.," I said. I was quiet the rest of the drive to the bus station. As the driver

pulled up to curb, I asked, "How much?"

"It's on me; it's the least I can do for you Sailor." He said.

At the bus terminal, another sailor in civvies told me he would stay at the restroom door, to watch my back, while I changed. After changing and purchasing my ticket, we sat together and realized we were traveling on the same bus. All I had with me was my carry on bag. The sea bag was checked for baggage shipment. My new acquaintance, whose name I cannot remember, was getting off the bus before me. Later that day he got off the bus; he was happy - he was home.

Sitting in the seat, I tried to relax, rest, and sleep to the smooth roll and sway of the ride. When I woke, it was dark. Most everyone else was sleeping. I mulled over the events of the day. Reliving the tensions, seeing the anger and distorted faces of the riotous crowd, I did not know how I would react if the same faces were seen at home.

The sun came up, night lights turned off, and the passengers started talking to each other. At a rest stop for breakfast, an older couple told me they could tell I was a serviceman by my haircut and offered to buy me my meal. They were very friendly. When they told me they lost their only son in Vietnam, I lost my appetite, but continued eating, slower. I told them how sorry I was for their loss. I tried to avoid them while they were on the bus. Whenever I heard of someone's loss, I thought how easily that could have been me.

The streets and buildings of Highland looked the same as when I left, but the people were different. Not like those raging idiots in California, but different. It took at least a week at home before the realization sunk in that the home people did not change. I had changed. What was important to them seemed somewhat frivolous to me. My priorities had changed. I was not the same person as when I left. I had matured and my perspective broadened.

My thinking was more we and us, than I and me. My chronological thinking was more months and years instead of now or today or this week.

After 30 days when my leave was up, I was reacquainted with old friends, making casual plans for the next leave. I had met a girl, who is now my wife, and dreams of settling down occupied my mind while bussing to OCS,

Officer Candidate School Staff, at Newport, Rhode Island.

Home Made Wine

Making homemade wine is an exercise in judgment. Do I make the wine sweet, semi-sweet, or dry? White or red? One variety or a blend of flavors and fruit? Carbonated or non-carbonated? High alcohol or low alcohol?

A family can legally make 200 gallons of wine for their own use, without paying tax, getting a license, or having revenue agents break down your door.

Our wine making is generally governed by the fruit grown on my property, and, or, what fruit is available. The time table is one that has been tested for hundreds of years. We generally put our own twist on it, so we can claim that it is our own concoction. Of course, if it turns out to be a bad batch, I say that the recipe was bad.

Usually, I like to make a wine from one fruit and then blend different wines to achieve the characteristics and taste I want. I have more control blending the finished wines than trying to blend the multiple fruits in one batch. We grow special grapes for the basic wines. Our best grape is a Buffalo grape, one that most people have never heard of, but to me is the best table and wine grape. The second grape is a Marsal Fock grape. We can never get a full crop because it is a small fruit, very sweet, and apparently addictive to birds. Usually, all we get are the skins, left after the bird flock raids. It seems they will peck their way through a steel wall to get to the Marsal Fock grape, once they are tasted. Other wines I make are: Sassafras, Bush Cherry,

Plum, Persimmon, Blackberry, Raspberry, Concord, and Meade.

Our wine is aged in five gallon stainless steel soda kegs that are charged with CO2. This eliminates oxidation from oxygen since Carbon-Dioxide is heavier than air and seals the wine. Also, the CO2 gives the wine a slight carbonation, improving its character.

I have taught many people to make their own wine. One in particular, my friend "Buddy", would never have a wine finish through the aging process. He would start drinking it during the secondary fermentation and it would all be gone before the aging process started. He said it was just too good to let it go any further.

Before I bought an automatic siphon, we would have to suck on a plastic hose to start the siphon transfer process. Sometimes we would hang onto the hose longer that what was needed to start the siphon action, just to make sure that the wine was ready, or good enough to keep, or decrease the number of bottles needed, or …..

We usually take one bottle and put a "Do not open prior to" date on it to make sure it gets aged for a proper amount of time. If it aged well, we will refer to our ledger of wines made, to replicate the recipe and any additional changes made to it.

We vary our methods between using hydrometer readings, to timing the different phases of wine making. Both methods work well, and both require maximum attention to a schedule. Others have told us of their wine making experiences. Some we learn from and other make us shudder, wondering how they can still be alive. We have heard how to make wine in the sun, to packing a wooden keg with grapes, nothing else, plugging the barrel and waiting a few years to drink the resulting liquid they call a vintage wine.

Well, I guess this article is finished. My wife called out to me to open a chilled bottle of wine and let it breath. She had just put a pizza in the oven.

The Wilding

The rabbit is just a few strides ahead, trying to lose me running through the underbrush and around obstacles. Leaping over the tangle of undergrowth I outsmart him. Leaning over to grab dinner, I hear a loud crack and feel a terrible pain across my back. Falling to the ground, my consciousness slowly slips away when I hear, "You damn fool, why did you have to shoot him?" I saw a hunter approach me and everything went black.

Pain courses over my back. My eyes slowly open. A fireplace is burning nearby throwing a blanket of heat over me. Trying to stand is useless, restraints keep me close to the floor. Water and food is within my reach, if I crawl. I feel safe, but from what I did not know, and I am frightened from the unknown.

The outside door slams open. A large hunter enters carrying firewood, and then puts the wood into a box next to the fireplace. Looking down at me, he approaches warily. Squatting down he holds out his hand and said, "How are we doing, big guy? My name is Jeb. I think you are going to be just fine. You just need a little TLC. Now don't struggle, you'll tear your wound open. Keep your eye on me while I fix myself something to eat. You'll see. I'm not going to hurt you." Getting up he starts a fire in a wood burning stove, then prepares meat and beans.

The smell of the frying meat makes my mouth water and makes me look over to the food and water. I crawl over and wolf down the food in the pan, and drink my fill of water. The pain seems to have lessened and a little of my nervousness left, but I still keep watching the huge man for any sudden or threatening motion. Exhaustion takes me into another sleep.

I wake to soft spoken words, "Okay, time to get up. You've been sleeping too long. You need some exercise or you'll get stiff."

Opening my eyes, I see the man with long hair. His heavy beard parted in a smile. He is wearing a coarse weave shirt with suspenders and loose fitting pants. His boots were made for the outdoors. He slowly lowers his hands to me, his eyes looking into mine. I do not feel threatened and let him slowly unbuckle my restraint. "Come on, get up. Try to stand." He slowly followed along side of me while I stagger around the room.

I make a full circle around the room, back to my pallet, where I again collapse from exhaustion. My restraints are not put back on and I will be able to move more freely. The food and water was refreshed, but I am too tired to go to it. The huge man goes about his chores looking at me occasionally while he talks in his soft and nurturing tone. Once, while I was lulled into a deep sleep, I woke to the gentle touch of his hand on me. It was a reassuring touch and I drifted back to sleep, feeling safe.

My sleep is restless, with dreams of danger and the call of the wild. Several times I wake thinking I hear someone calling me. I would lie still, listening intently, but could only hear the nightlife outside. I wake early, hours before sunrise, and slowly walk around the room softly, easily seeing everything with my excellent night vision and investigate all that interests me. I stand by the man's bed studying him while he slept. I could have left then, but I want to find out more about this caring man. After viewing everything in the room, I return to my bed on the floor and wait for daybreak. While waiting for the man to awake, I flex my muscles, stretching them to regain my strength. The wound is starting to knit and I am careful not to over extend my activities.

The sun is starting to burn the treetops when Jeb stirred. He looks over, noticed I was staring at him. "Looks like someone is feeling better this morning. Are you up for a walk outside?" I rise to my feet and carefully follow him to the door and outside.

Jeb sat on a chair and motioned me off the porch with a wave of his hand. "Go on, do your thing now. I may not be here to let you out when the urge comes."

I walk down the two steps and out onto the grass. I find a suitable spot and relieve myself. I walk around taking in the sights, sounds, and smells. Satisfied with the area, I return to the porch to sit and watch Jeb rock in the chair.

Later that day, I follow Jeb do his outside chores. I take particular interest in the chickens, but he closed the door when entering the coop and they did not see me. Jeb came out the door with a small bucket of eggs. "Not for you," he said. Those eggs look pretty good to me. I could feel my mouth water, and thought I could taste the eggs. We went back to the cabin. Jeb went in with the eggs and I stayed on the porch slumbering in the warm sunshine.

The closing door wakes me and Jeb is bringing my food and water out on the porch. I wonder if I have lost my bed by the warm fireplace. The daylight is turning to dusk when Jeb opens the door to go inside. I stand still watching him to see what I should do. "Come on," he said. I answer with a wag of my tail.

Later he brings my food and water back inside. I lick his hand to let him know I am happy with him. I follow him to a chair where he sits and examines my wound. "You're healing nicely. Now I have to come up with a name for you. What do you think about Wolf? That's a good name since you're a wolf, Wolf." Jeb chuckled, then petted me obviously pleased with himself on naming me wolf.

Weeks pass, my wound heals and strength returns. Jeb feeds me and I guard the cabin at night and warn him of approaching animals or dangers during the day. We become a team with trust in each other. I still enjoy watching the chickens, but Jeb is diligent about closing the coop door. I try to let him know when he is taking eggs back to the cabin that I really like eggs, but he is very careful not to let them in my reach. I also like the chickens, but he knows better than to let the coop door open and he let me know that the chickens are off limits to me. There is no doubt that he knows, that I know, that there are no chickens for me.

A little past sunrise, I am sprawled on the porch, guarding the door, when a new man came out of the woods. He has a pack of skins on his back and carrying a gun. There is something about him that I do not like. My growl alerts Jeb and he opens the door. The new man hails Jeb like he knows him. I do not care, I still dislike the man. Approaching the porch he said. "I see you nursed that wolf back to health. I heard about it at the post. You must not have a brain in your head."

I look at Jeb, asking him with my growls, what he wants me to do. "Easy Wolf. Everything's Okay." "Jake, you don't have to concern yourself with Wolf. He's the best friend I have. It's you I have to worry about. I hear you've been making bad kills and not running your traps like you should. I hear you're letting the beaver rot in your traps. That's not the way you were taught."

I look at the new man; see his face flush like the evening sun. His lips snarl in a language I understood.

"No one can talk to me like that. I'll kill that damn nuisance animal now. You don't control my life and what I do." The new man swings the rifle from his shoulder toward me.

Jeb yells, "No." Jumping forward, Jeb trips, falling down in front of me. I hear a crack. A noise I heard once before. Blood spatters onto my face. Before Jeb stopped rolling, I leapt at the new man. My lunge knocks the rifle from his hands, and throws him to the ground. My teeth clamp onto his throat in a death grip. Snorts and gasps come from his nose and mouth. His arms flail about my body, but he can not dislodge my grip. Soon his body starts shaking, then stills.

Crawling from his chest, I go to Jeb. His is on the ground not moving. His breathing is shallow and steady. I lick his face trying to wake him. Finally his eyes open. Jeb rolls over and I see blood on the front and back of his shoulder. "Wolf, help me into the cabin." Jeb gets to his hands and knees but can not stand up. Throwing his arm over my back, he tests my strength by putting some of his weight on me. The weight is more than I have ever carried and I am surprised I can hold him up. Together we crawl into the cabin, over to his bunk, and I help him up and in. Putting my paws on the bed rail, I try to lick his wound, but his shirt had shifted and is covering it. Lopping to the sink, I pull down the towel still wet from the morning wash and give it to Jeb. He slowly unbuttons his shirt and carefully wipes his wound clean. He can barely hold his eyes open. Running to the table I pick up his unfinished morning coffee. My tongue slips into the fowl tasting liquid, but I continue to carry it to Jeb. Raising myself to the bed rail, I sit the tin cup on Jeb's chest, waiting for him to get a firm hold on it.

Jeb drinks, spilling some on his chest, then drops the cup on the floor. I pick up the cup and put it back on the table. I pick up some biscuits left over from breakfast, taking them back to Jeb, laying them down next to him on the blanket. His eyes are closed and I can hear his breathing.

He has somehow placed the wet towel over his shoulder, covering the wound, front and back. He needs his rest. Going back outside, I check the new man. Yes, he is still dead. Struggling with the dead weight, I manage to roll the dead man sideways, down the dropping yard to the creek at the bottom of the hill, near the woods. Hopefully, running water will float him down stream to feed the timber dwellers.

I return to my post on the porch. The evening chill is dropping down off the mountain. On my way to the wood box, I check on Jeb. He is sleeping soundly. I select some of the smaller pieces of wood and toss them one by one into the slumbering fire. Once in the fireplace, I cannot reposition them. They will have to stay where they land. I check that there were no embers outside the fire box on the stoop or floor. Jeb would never be able to escape a burning cabin. I man, or rather wolf, my post at the door. I check on Jeb throughout the night whenever I hear groans or Jeb talking in his sleep.

Sunrise shines through the front door and windows. I try to dip water out of the bucket, but cannot stand tall enough to gain access to the top with the dipper's long handle. Wanting to somehow help, I go to Jeb and lick his face. I smell and taste the sweat and strain he slept through. I cannot wipe the taste off my tongue, before going to my water bowl to drink and wash it off.

I stay with Jeb while he recovers, bringing him wild game to prepare and eat. During the nights my pack brothers call for me, but I must stay until Jeb is well. I stay at his side during the day, letting him rest his hand on my head and back. This seems to comfort him. One day he gets up and goes outside to draw a fresh bucket of water. Heating some water he washed and shaved. I knew he was almost ready to be on his own. I continued to bring him wild game, and I did stop to watch the chickens when passing their coop. They have gotten use to me, and do not run around squawking, running back into their coop. I have not yet figured out a way to get to the eggs, maybe someday.

Jeb went outside and cut kindling and I know he is fully recovered. That night I answer my pack brothers and join them in the hunt. I return to Jeb daily to check up on him and to let him know I am around. My visits with him slowly decrease, but I always watch him while hiding in the wood. I know he thinks of me, because my food and water is always fresh sitting beside the door on the porch, at night, after patrolling around the cabin. I always leave my scent to ward off the predators that might pass in the night.

One evening I came to the cabin early, and a new scent reaches out to me. I stand on my hind feet to look in the window. There is someone in the cabin talking to Jeb. A tall woman is cleaning and washing. I can tell from her scent and the

sound of her voice, that she will be good for Jeb.
I will not have to worry about him anymore.

The Seven Gates of Hell

It was just a dare. How did I know that it would change my life forever? I thought the legend was just folklore, not something real. What happened to me only happens in scary movies, or old stories told around a camp fire.

It all started when an article **"The Gates of Hell" – History of A Local Legend**, ran in the Troy Times Tribune about the legend. I remember the day, or rather the evening perfectly. It was Thursday, October 28, 2010. We had family visiting and joked about the legend. What a great experience it would be to take my grandchildren through the seven gates and in the proper sequence. That would give my grandkids something to talk about for many years to come.

I gathered the kids around and in the scariest voice I could muster, asked if they would like to pass through The Seven Gates of Hell? Dyllan, Travis, Nicole, Austin, and Cassidy were excited at the thought of doing what very few had done. They could see themselves telling the story to their friends at school. They would be **COOL**. We had already experienced walking through the cemetery on Halloween Eve to tempt the spirits, but this would top anything we did before.

I read more of the article to everyone. The "Gates of Hell" are a series of seven underpasses beneath old rail lines on rural back roads between Troy and Collinsville, Illinois. The underpasses had been named gates due to the resemblance to the large entrances in walls that surround castles.

The junction of pathway crossings have always been seen as superstitious, magical or mystical in many of the world cultures going back to the beginning of time. They are also symbolic because they are neither here nor there. Another dark connection is that they were often used to bury executed criminals or people who had committed suicide.

Crossroads have also been meeting places for secret societies and where people supposedly performed magic.

These gates of hell also held a legend of a death by hanging. A young man was supposedly in love with a young woman and was murdered by a rival suitor. Another story states that he hung himself in shame after committing a murder. And lastly, he was hung by the Ku Klux Klan. Some of ground surrounding several of the gates is rumored to be secret meeting places of the KKK.

Black magic is reported to be practiced at the gates, with tales of animal sacrifice and other rituals witnessed by anonymous people. It is also reported that "Hell Hounds" guard the gates from anyone who may visit too long, or seem to be investigating the surrounding areas.

Supporting the legends is the fact that the roads passing through the gates are dangerous to those that navigate them with inattentiveness. The winding roadways and hidden curves turning into some of the gates are very unforgiving. The secluded areas are also a welcoming place for those who need a place for doing drugs and the hallucinations the illicit substances produce.

To properly antagonize the subterranean denizens, one must pass through the gates in the correct order. From U.S. Route 40, drive south Through back roads until you come into downtown Collinsville. Caution is stressed as the road are narrow with many blind turns, especially at the two gates.

At this point, you have two options. 1.- Drive back the way you came, through all seven gates to cancel invoking the curse, or 2.- return home on a more doable road. Needless to say, I took the easy way returning home.

The next evening I was driving out of my driveway, which is a very short distance from the Cemetery when I heard an eerie howling from a pack of canines. I had never heard animals sounding like that before. Goosebumps popped, tremors traveled down my spine, and my hair stood up on end. As my headlights swung out onto Lower Marine Road, I saw multiple flaming red spots fifty foot ahead. Driving closer I could see the spots were reflections from the eyes of huge wolves – there are no wolves around here. Fear drove me to increase my speed as I knew stopping was impossible. They scattered as I drove through them. No bumps, no screams, no anything. They just seemed to evaporate around me, but not before staring at me through the windshield and side windows. The teeth were huge and their mouths appeared to be smiling with drool stringing down out of sight. A few appeared to float along with me for a while, as I continued driving.

Returning home from Wal-Mart with the groceries bought, I wanted to take a different route home, but habit controlled the car. I slowed at my neighbor's house, just before the encounter spot. Giving a sigh of relief and hoping the sweat would dry before arriving home, I continued driving.

Opening the car door and while reaching in to pick up the bag of groceries, I felt a huge weight hit my back. Teeth savagely attacked the back of my neck. Falling over backwards, another weight landed on my chest while long white teeth tore at my neck. Fangs were tearing at me from every direction. I was being ripped apart. A welcomed blackness followed.

My waking was unremarkable. No blood, no torn flesh. My clothes were mussed and a little dirty from being on the ground. The groceries were easily picked up and rebagged. I seemed to have a keener sense of the surrounding environment. My sense of smell was more acute. My muscles more toned. Knees no longer hurt when walking were now youthful and I had a spring in my step.

My wife had taken a nap while I was gone and did not notice the time span from when I left. She did notice my more youthful bearing and stated that I must be exercising more without her.

Now I dread the full moon or hearing a far off howl commanding my presence participate in surreal ceremonies or assume gate guard duties. I worry that some telling hair might remain on me, revealing what I have become. I pray when I can, that my soul is not damned and that whatever I have become is reversible. I pray when I can.

About The Author

Charles "Chuck" Schwend served 20 years in the U.S. Navy, retiring as a Chief Petty Officer. Some of the many military positions held were, B-26 (JD-1) crewmember; Foreign National Recruiter under the U.S. State Department; U.S. Navy and U.S. Coast Guard Recruiter for the Far East; U.S. Navy Liaison to the U.S. Army; Personnel Casualty Control, Cruiser – Destroyer Force, Atlantic Fleet, etc. Journalism major at SIU-E, Museology Specialization at SIE-U-E. Co-founded the Highland League of Writers Group, Highland, Illinois. Retired from the State of Illinois. Leisure activities include, writing; beekeeping; wine making; cordial making; and mushroom cultivation.

www.ingramcontent.com/pod-product-compliance
Lightning Source LLC
Chambersburg PA
CBHW050735250626
47155CB00005B/1781